I0547511

DEEPER YOU DIG

Lost Kings MC #21.5

AUTUMN JONES LAKE

COPYRIGHT

Deeper You Dig: A Lost Kings MC Halloween
© 2022 Autumn Jones Lake All rights reserved
Digital ISBN: 978-1-943950-87-4
Paperback ISBN: 978-1-943950-88-1
Proofreading: Julie Barney
Cover design: Autumn Jones Lake

This is a work of fiction. The Lost Kings MC, names, characters, places, and incidents are the product of the author's imagination. Any resemblance to actual people, alive or dead, business, establishments, or events is entirely coincidental. Any reference to real events, business, organizations, or locales is intended only to give the story a sense of realism and authenticity. No part of this publication may be reproduced, stored in a retrieval system, or transmitted by any means – electronic, mechanical, photographic, recording, or otherwise – without prior permission from the author. Lost Kings MC and Autumn Jones Lake are registered trademarks.

The author acknowledges the copyrighted or trademarked status and trademark owners of the word marks mentioned in this work of fiction.

ABOUT DEEPER YOU DIG

USA Today bestselling author Autumn Jones Lake delivers a fun and spooky installment of the Lost Kings MC series.

Trick-or-treat! It's time for the grand opening of the new clubhouse...

Ravage has been tasked with planning the Halloween party this year. Everyone will be there wearing their creepiest and most creative costumes. An unexpected treat leads to a brush with death that wasn't in Ravage's plans.

Catch up with your favorite couples and gain insight about some mysterious members of the Lost Kings Motorcycle Club in this Halloween-themed novella.

ALSO BY AUTUMN JONES LAKE

THE LOST KINGS MC™ SERIES

Slow Burn (Lost Kings MC #1)– *Free ebook!*

Corrupting Cinderella (Lost Kings MC #2)

Three Kings, One Night (Lost Kings MC #2.5)

Strength From Loyalty (Lost Kings MC #3)

Tattered on My Sleeve (Lost Kings MC #4)

White Heat (Lost Kings MC #5)

Between Embers (Lost Kings MC #5.5)

More Than Miles (Lost Kings MC #6)

White Knuckles (Lost Kings MC #7)

Beyond Reckless (Lost Kings MC #8)

Beyond Reason (Lost Kings MC #9)

One Empire Night (Lost Kings MC #9.5)

After Burn (Lost Kings MC #10)

After Glow (Lost Kings MC #11)

Zero Hour (Lost Kings MC #11.5) - *Free ebook!*

Zero Tolerance (Lost Kings MC #12)

Zero Regret (Lost Kings MC #13)

Zero Apologies (Lost Kings MC #14)

White Lies (Lost Kings MC #15)

Swagger and Sass (A Lost Kings MC Novella) - *Free ebook!*

Rhythm of the Road (Lost Kings MC #16)

Lyrics on the Wind (Lost Kings MC #17)

Diamond in the Dust (Lost Kings MC #18)

Crown of Ghosts (Lost Kings MC #19)
Throne of Scars (Lost Kings MC #20)
Reckless Truths (Lost Kings MC #21)
Deeper You Dig (Lost Kings MC #21.5)
Rust or Ride (Lost Kings MC #22)
...and many more to come!

BOOKS IN THE LOST KINGS MC WORLD
The Hollywood Demons Series
Kickstart My Heart
Blow My Fuse
Wheels of Fire

Bullets & Bonfires
Warnings & Wildfires
Renegade Path

Paranormal Romance
Catnip & Cauldrons
Onyx Night
Onyx Shadows
Feral Escape

GLOSSARY OF CHARACTERS

The Lost Kings MC™ World © Autumn Jones Lake

If you haven't read the series in a little while, here is a quick rundown of characters relevant to Deeper You Dig, so you can enjoy this fun little read without wondering who is who.

THE LOST KINGS MC: UPSTATE, NY
"EMPIRE," NY

- **President:** Rochlan "Rock" North. Leader of the Upstate NY charter of the Lost Kings MC.
- **Sergeant-at-Arms:** Wyatt "Wrath" Ramsey. Protector or enforcer for the club.
- **Vice President:** Blake "Murphy" O'Callaghan. Murphy was the road captain up until *White Lies* (*Lost Kings MC #15*) He's now the Vice President and getting adjusted to his new responsibilities within the club.

- **Treasurer:** Marcel "Teller" Whelan. Handles the money and investments for the club. Engaged to Charlotte. Rock's unknown son up until *After Glow* (*Lost Kings MC #11*). In *Reckless Truths* (*Lost Kings MC #21*) the whole club found out about their relationship.
- **Road Captain:** Dixon "Dex" Watts (newly appointed to the position in *White Lies*) His full story will be available in 2023.
- **Grayson "Grinder" Lock:** The former sergeant-at-arms of the New York charter. We saw a little about his relationship as Rock's mentor in *Wheels of Fire* (*Hollywood Deoms #3*). We first "met" him in *Corrupting Cinderella* (*Lost Kings MC #2*) and have seen him a few other times throughout the series, most recently in *Zero Regret* (*Lost Kings MC #13*.) He has been mentioned throughout the series by the brothers as they looked forward to his release from prison. He was voted in as the SAA for the downstate charter in *Throne of Scars*.

THE LOST KINGS MC: DOWNSTATE, NY "UNION" NY

- **President:** Angus "Zero" or "Z" Frazier. As of *Zero Apologies* (*Lost Kings MC #14*), Z is the president of the Downstate, NY charter of the Lost Kings MC.

- **Vice President:** Logan "Rooster" Randall, the cocky bearded man who stole Shelby Morgan's heart.
- **Sergeant-at-Arms:** Grayson "Grinder" Lock as of *Throne of Scars*.
- **Treasurer:** Hustler
- **Road Captain:** Jensen "Jigsaw" Kilgore, Has a younger sister named Jezzie who we haven't met yet.

Other Lost Kings MC Members

Thomas "Ravage" Kane: We've gotten to know Rav and his snarky humor a little bit better in each book. Ravage is a general member who helps out wherever he is needed. As of *Reckless Truths*, he was tasked with organizing events at the new clubhouse in Empire.

Cronin "Sparky" Petek: Sparky is the mad genius/hippie stoner behind the Lost Kings MC's pot-growing business. He is rarely seen outside of the basement, as he prefers the company of his plants.

Elias "Bricks" Serrano: We have seen Bricks and his girlfriend Winter throughout the series. He's one of the few members who does not live at the clubhouse.

Sam "Stash" Black: Lives in the basement with Sparky and helps with the plants.

Hoot: We've seen glimpses of him since *Slow Burn* when he was a lowly prospect. He finally got his full patch, but still gets a lot of the grunt work. In Reckless Truths we discovered he has some interesting...hardware.

Birch: We also met him as a prospect. He's been voted as a full-patch member but shares in a lot of the grunt work with Hoot.

The Ladies Of The Lost Kings MC

Hope Kendall North, Esq.: Former lawyer. Nicknamed *First Lady* by Murphy in *Corrupting Cinderella* (*Lost Kings MC* #2), Hope is the object of Rock's love and obsession. Their daughter is named Grace after Rock's mother.

Trinity Hurst Ramsey: Wrath's angel. Former caretaker of the club. She now has her own photography and graphic design business. She is married to Wrath, fiercely loyal to the club, and best friends with Hope.

Heidi "Little Hammer" O'Callaghan: Murphy's wife and Teller's little sister. Heidi just graduated from college and works at Empire Med. Murphy officially adopted her daughter, Alexa Jade in White Lies.

Charlotte Clark, Esq: Teller's Sunshine. Lawyer. Married Teller in *Reckless Truths*. Often credited with taming the brooding treasurer of the Lost Kings. Currently pregnant with twins.

Lilly Frazier: Z's brave and devoted siren. The new

queen of the Lost Kings MC's downstate charter. One of Hope's best friends. Z and Lilly's son is named Chance.

Shelby Morgan: Rooster's sassy little chickadee. Country music singer from Texas. We first met Shelby in *Swagger and Sass*. In *Diamond in the Dust*, she moved to New York to be with Rooster when she's not on the road. She loves flamingos, flamingo puns, and tarot cards.

Serena Cargill: Former downstate club girl. At one time, she was broken-hearted over Murphy. We first met her in *Strength From Loyalty*, got to know her better in *White Heat* and *More Than Miles*. She has appeared here and there in the series since then. Mistreated by Shadow, the former VP of the downstate charter, we had not "seen" her since *Zero Regret*. Then she healed Grinder's heart *in Crown of Ghosts/Throne of Scars*. She loves makeup and runs a YouTube channel where she posts makeup tutorials. Has gotten to be good friends with Shelby. Is currently pregnant with baby Lincoln.

Swan: Lost Kings MC club girl and dancer at Crystal Ball. Swan has found a new calling as the yoga teacher for the old ladies of the Lost Kings MC and is slowly moving away from dancing.

Other Recurring Characters Relevant To This Story

Carter Clark: Charlotte's goofy, often inappropriate, younger brother. He lives in a guest house on Charlotte and

Teller's property. He helps babysit the club's kids sometimes and started a job tattooing with Bronze. He also works for Rock at his custom bike shop. In Reckless Truths, Wrath gifted him with the nickname "Scribbles" as a nod to his artistic talent. May or may not be seeing Swan.

Jake Wallace: One of Wrath's business partners in Furious Fitness. Jake has appeared off and on throughout the series since *Tattered on my Sleeve*. He sometimes holds self-defense classes for the ladies. He's the younger brother of Sullivan Wallace, whose story can be found in Warnings & Wildfires.

Remington "Ruthless" Holt: Owns "The Castle" with his best friend, Griff. It's an underground fighting ring Murphy used to participate in. We've seen him most recently in *White Lies and Lyrics on the Wind*. Remy is the caretaker of his younger sister, Molly. He is currently considering forming a support club to the Lost Kings MC with Griff, Eraser, and Vapor.

Griffin "Stonewall" Royal: Remy's best friend and business partner. We saw him most recently in *Lyrics on the Wind*.

Eraser: Owns Zips, a racetrack near the Lost Kings MC territory. Married to Ella.

Roman "Vapor" Hawkins: The book *Renegade Path* is his story. We first met him and his wife, Juliet, in *After Burn*.

Lynn Morgan: Shelby's mother.

Lost Kings MC Terminology

LOKI: Short for LOst KIngs

War room: Where the Lost Kings hold "church."

Property patch: When a member takes a woman as his old lady (wife status), he gives her a vest with a property patch. In my series, the vest has a "Property of Lost Kings MC" patch and the member's road name on the back. The officers also place their patches on the ol' lady's vest as a sign that they always have her back. Her man's patch or club symbol is placed over the heart. Rock's patch is a crown. Wrath's is a star. Murphy's is a four-leaf clover. Teller's is a dollar sign. Z's is the letter Z. Rooster's is a rooster wearing a crown. As a joke, Wrath gave Rock and Hope a "product of" patch for baby Grace. Maybe it will catch on as more kids are born into the club? We'll see.

PLACES IN THE LOST KINGS MC WORLD

I use a mix of real and imaginary names to describe the places in my series. Again, I bend and shape geography to my needs as this is a *fictional world that I have created.*

Crystal Ball: The strip club owned by the Lost Kings MC and one of their legitimate businesses. They often refer to it simply as "CB." Located in Empire County.

Furious Fitness: The gym Wrath owns. Often just referred to as "Furious." Located not far from Crystal Ball.

Empire, NY: The territory run by the Lost Kings MC

upstate charter. This is a fictional version of Albany, NY, the capital of New York State. Many of the Lost Kings MC's businesses are located in and around Empire.

Slater, NY: Loosely based on Schenectady County. Until recently it was the Wolf Knights MC's territory. The Lost Kings MC will be taking control of Slater.

Ironworks, NY: Loosely based on Rensselaer County (Troy, NY). In the beginning of the series, it was run by the Vipers MC. It is now considered territory of the Lost Kings MC.

Union, NY: A fictional area two hours south of Empire, NY, where the "downstate" charter is located.

Strike Back: Owned by Sullivan Wallace but members of the Lost Kings MC have worked there in the past.

Johnson County/Johnsonville: Fictional area where Heidi grew up. About an hour west of "Empire." Where Strike Back Gym, The Castle, and Zips are located. Possibly the new home of a Lost Kings MC support club? We'll see!

Zips: Racetrack owned by Eraser where all the illegal gambling/racing in the area happens.

The Castle: Formerly a juvenile detention center. The building is now used to house the underground fighting ring run by Remy and Griff. Murphy used to fight here. Other LOKI members also blow off steam in the cage here from time to time. Located in the middle of nowhere, NY, it once-upon-a-time housed Griff, Vapor, and possibly Teller during their "troubled youth" days.

OTHER MC TERMINOLOGY

Most terminology was obtained through research. However, I have also used some artistic license in applying these terms to my romanticized, fictional version of an outlaw motorcycle club. This is not an exhaustive list.

Cage: A car, truck, van—basically anything other than a motorcycle.

Church: Club meetings all full-patch members must attend. Led by the president of the club, but officers will update the members on the areas they oversee. (Some clubs refer to the meeting room where they hold church as the "chapel." My club refers to it as their "war room."

Citizen: Anyone not a hardcore biker or belonging to an outlaw club. "Citizen wife" would refer to a spouse kept entirely separate from the club.

Cut: Leather vest worn by outlaw bikers and adorned with patches and artwork displaying the club's unique colors. The Lost Kings' colors are blue and gray. Their logo is a skull with a crown. The *Respect Few, Fear None* patch is earned by doing time for the club without snitching. *Brother's Keeper* patches are earned by killing for the club. *Loyal Brother* is for a brother who's spent more than five years with the club.

Muffler bunny or "bunnies": A girl who hangs around to provide sexual favors to members. Old ladies in my series will sometimes refer to them as "friends of the club," depending on the girl in question. Some clubs refer to them as club whores, patch whores, or cut sluts. These terms are not regularly used in my series. Sometimes simply referred to as a "club girl."

Nomad: A club member who does not belong to any specific charter, yet has privileges in all charters.

Old lady/ol' lady: Wife or steady girlfriend of a club member.

Patched in: When a new member is approved for full membership.

Patch holder: A member who has been vetted through performing duties for the club as a prospect or probate and has earned his three-piece patch.

Road name: Nickname. Usually given by the other members.

Run: A club-sanctioned outing, sometimes with other chapters and/or clubs. Can also refer to a club business run.

I'm sure I'm forgetting something! But that should get you started!

DEDICATION

To those who enjoy laughter with their screams.

CHAPTER ONE
Wrath

TWO WEEKS BEFORE HALLOWEEN...

There are times and situations that require a hard dick. At the table during church isn't one of them.

I never should've watched Trinity wriggle into a Halloween costume before leaving our house to go to the clubhouse. She didn't tell me what exactly she was supposed to be. It didn't matter—the outfit was sexy as fuck. The picture she sent me right before I took my seat didn't free up any room behind my fly either.

Rock's fingers cross my vision, snapping together.

Once.

Twice.

"You with us?" he asks with an edge of annoyance only Rock can get away with.

"What?" I shift in my chair. Slowly, the war room comes into focus as I blink away the image of Trinity squeezing her ample curves into shiny, white leather.

"As I was saying." Teller glares at me from his seat across the table.

Glare all you want, welterweight.

"I think the best location for this charity event would be Furious."

"You want to shut down the gym for a day so a bunch of little snot-monsters can run around?" He can't be serious.

"It's a big favor," Teller concedes. "But Crystal Ball isn't exactly a great location for a kids' event."

Normally I'd say it's better to collect favors than hand them out. Except when it comes to my brothers. Fuckers know I'll do anything for the club.

Doesn't mean I won't enjoy being a dick about it.

"Why exactly am I going to turn half of Furious Fitness into a kiddie carnival?" I raise my eyebrows and stare Dex and Z—the two geniuses responsible for this idea—down.

"Haunted house," Z corrects.

"Dibs on the pumpkin carving station." Jigsaw zigzags his hunting knife through the air to demonstrate his talents.

"Easy, Michael Myers," Z says, holding out his hands like a lion tamer. "I don't know if stabby utensils are the way to go on this event."

Teller snort-chuckles into his fist. "Michael Myers my ass. More like Pennywise." He leans over the table to lift his chin at Jigsaw. "What the fuck you wearing, bro?"

Sparky shivers and squeezes his eyes shut. "Pennywise is fuckin' scary. I hate clowns."

"Weird, since you *are* a clown," Stash mutters.

Jigsaw flicks the ties of the frilly black shirt he's wearing under his cut. "I'm thinking of attending this year's festivities as a pirate."

"Halloween isn't for two more weeks," Rooster mutters.

Z sits forward, resting his elbows on the table and pins Jigsaw with a stern look. "You thought church was a good place for your costume trial run?"

"Yeah." Jigsaw grins at Z at one end of the table, then at Rock at the opposite end. "Why not?"

"I think he doesn't want to admit this was a serious fashion choice." Murphy squints at Jigsaw and pretends to give his outfit a closer inspection. "Did you steal that from an ol' lady's closet? I swear Heidi has a blouse that looks just like that."

I snicker and reach across the table to bump my knuckles against Murphy's.

"Z's right," Dex says, putting an end to us picking on Jigsaw. "We used to do a lot more charity events in Empire. It wouldn't hurt to slap a fresh coat of paint on our 'nothing but good guys who ride Harleys' reputation. With all the shit going on with MCs in other areas, we should dust off our warm, fuzzy sides and show them off."

"Thank you for volunteering, *warm fuzzy*." I reach for a pen and piece of paper. "'Dex—in charge of haunted house.'"

"No way," Ravage protests. "John Wick over there might scare the kids away."

Dex shoots him a glare, then turns toward me. "I'll have my hands full with Crystal Ball on Halloween, brother. It's one of our busiest nights."

Fuck, he's right. Dex has enough to do.

"Maybe Murphy should do it," Z suggests.

"Since he's basically an overgrown child?" Teller asks.

"Fuck yeah, I'll decorate the shit out of Furious." Murphy sends me a big shit-eating grin, daring me to make fun of him.

Sometimes I miss the days when he feared me. "Just because we're partners and you're wearing that VP patch now doesn't mean I won't kick your ass."

"Bring it on, big guy." He motions to me with his fingers.

Just as I lean over the table to wrap my fingers around his throat, Rock stops me with a hand to my chest. "Simmer the fuck down."

Bricks raises his hand. "I'll do it." He leans forward to get Teller's attention. "Think Scribbles would be willing to help out?"

"Yeah, Carter would probably be down for that," Teller says, then flicks his gaze my way.

"What?" I ask.

"Trinity's an artist too. Think she'll want to work on it?"

I'm not usually a fan of anyone volunteering my wife for free labor. But I'd rather have Trinity oversee this project. She won't let anyone fuck up my gym beyond repair. Plus, I know damn well how excited she'll be to flex her creative muscles. "Probably. I'll ask her."

"Swan's head of the decorating committee at Crystal Ball," Dex volunteers. "I'm sure she'll help out if Trinity doesn't have time."

"Skip the apple-bobbing this year," Z says to Dex.

"Remember when we set that up and Annie tried to drown that other chick?"

Dex smirks. "How could I forget."

"What about you, Farmer Bob?" Z lifts his chin at Teller. "Lilly said you're arranging something at your doomsday compound."

Teller rolls his eyes. "For the little guys, not for *you*. Carter and I have been working on a mini hay bale maze in the backyard. If you decide on a maze at Furious, he'll be prepared." He turns toward Rock. "We're not planning to scare the shit out of the kids or anything spooky. So it'll be safe for Grace."

Rock nods. "Thanks."

Teller leans forward again, staring down the table at Bricks. "You and Winter should bring the little guys over, too."

"I dunno, man. Deacon informed me that he's 'too big' for trick-or-treating this year," Bricks laughs.

"He can help me 'manage' the little guys if he wants," Teller offers.

"Thanks, bro."

"Kiddie mazes?" Ravage drums his fingers on the table. "We all got called to the table for this?"

"Fuck off," Teller grumbles. "Sorry if we interrupted your riveting day of jacking off and playing video games."

Ravage jerks his fist in the air, as if he wants to prove he's a jack-off expert. Sparky jumps out of his chair and shoves Ravage, almost knocking him onto the floor.

"Have some respect." Sparky settles into his seat again.

Ravage stares at him but keeps his mouth shut.

I catch Rock's eye and he shakes his head.

"All right." Rock smacks the gavel down. "Charity events are club business." He sends a pointed look Rav's way. "Showing a good face to our local community is every brother's responsibility."

"Rav doesn't have a good face. Just that sorry one," Z says.

"Ladies love my face." Rav sticks out his tongue.

"What charity are we donating the funds to?" Rock asks, ignoring the interruptions.

"The help-homely-bikers-get-laid project?" Hoot suggests.

"Watch it," Rav warns. "You ain't that far away from your prospecting days."

Hoot holds up his hands in surrender. "Kinda weird you assumed I was talking about you."

"How about a local food pantry?" Sparky says, ignoring Hoot asserting himself. "Willow says they're all hurting right now."

"Good one." Rock glances around the table, checking that everyone agrees. He leans over to Teller and taps the notepad in front of him. "Club will match whatever we raise."

"Okay." Teller nods.

Once he's satisfied with our chosen charity, Rock lifts his chin at Z. "Want to name a second organization?"

Z sweeps his gaze over his guys and Rooster raises his hand. "How about Dream Makers? Shelby works with them to visit kids in the hospital, but they also have a separate charity that helps families directly with housing and stuff while the kids are in the hospital getting treatment. She says they're always looking for help. Plus, they've got homes in both Union and Empire."

"Yeah, that's a good one," Z says.

"Sounds perfect," Rock adds. "Thanks, Rooster."

"No one's gonna be bitchy about receiving money from an MC, right?" Ravage asks.

Teller shrugs. "We can donate under one of our corporate entities."

"Doesn't that defeat the purpose of showing a good face to the community and all that?" Butcher asks.

Rock sits back, I think pleased that one of Z's guys said something dumb for once.

Z lets out a long sigh. "Some good press would be nice but I'm also fine with it being anonymous." He shrugs. "We should do some good where we live. Even if we don't get credit."

"Speak for yourself," I say. "I already opened my business to—"

"Delinquents who remind you of yourself?" Z finishes.

"Fuck off," I growl. He's probably right but what-the-fuck-ever.

Hustler raises his hand. "I'm down with the charity stuff. But what are we doing at night?" He turns bright, deviant eyes Dex's way. "Can we celebrate at the new clubhouse? Maybe some of the dancers can come over when CB closes."

"Yeah," Dex answers slowly, "I'm sure after a night of

strenuous work and fending off handsy old farts, they'd love to come entertain you."

"Fuck yeah." Ravage punches his fist in the air, then points down the table at Rock. "You promised me Halloween, Prez. I'm putting an epic party together." He stands and scans the table, meeting each of our eyes. "I expect every brother to be there. Even the neutered, married ones."

Grinder has been silent during all the fuckery. But now, he sits forward and narrows his eyes. "Who're you calling neutered?"

Ravage backs a step away from the table. "Brothers and ol' ladies are invited," he says in a wounded tone. As if the lack of an invitation was Grinder's issue. "I want everyone to see the new clubhouse."

"If we've already seen it, can we skip it?" I ask, raising my hand to increase the asshole factor.

"No!" Rav all but stamps his damn foot on the floor.

"Bro, you're being creepy. You plannin' to drug us and handcuff us to a wall in the basement or something?" Murphy asks.

"Don't give him ideas," Rooster whispers, loud enough for all of us to hear.

"Rav's right." Rock stops for a long breath as if he can't believe the words marching out of his mouth. "I expect every upstate brother to make an appearance."

Rock's word may be the law around here, but I still want to put my fist in his throat for ordering us to attend Rav's party.

"Uh, Rock," Dex says. "I'll come over after CB closes, but it'll be late—"

"You've already been there plenty of times," Rock says. "You're excused." He looks down the table at Z. "Obviously, the invitation is extended to our downstate brothers as well."

Z grins. "Great. I expect every single one of you fucks to be at this party, too." He nods at Rav. "That little chucklefuck campaigned hard for the new clubhouse so all you assholes can have a child-free zone to crash at when you're up here visiting."

Rav preens like a horny peacock.

"Uh..." Rooster raises his hand. "I'd like to crash at the man-child-free zone if that's all right with you."

Z glares at him.

"Fine." Rooster rolls his eyes. "Shelby was working on a costume anyway." He glances at Grinder and smirks. "She and Serena were brainstorming costumes together."

A smile twitches at the corners of Grinder's mouth. "I know what both of them chose."

Ravage presses his palms together like he's praying to the lord of deviant bikers. "Please let them be slutty."

Rooster jumps up, knocking his chair backward.

I smother laughter behind my fist.

"Say that again," Rooster challenges.

"What?" Ravage's eyes widen as he backs up. "It's a legit category of costume." He searches the table for someone to agree with him. "You know, slutty nurse, slutty teacher," for some reason he shoots a pleading look at Teller, "slutty lawyer?"

"Are you out of your fucking mind?" Teller growls.

"Wrath should go as the Jolly Green Giant," Sparky suggests, shooting a worried frown at Ravage, then Teller.

"Why?" Dex smirks at me. "He's neither jolly nor green." I clap my hands together with a crisp smack. "How 'bout I go as someone who cracks your skull like an egg?" I point at Rav, so it's clear I'm not threatening Dex.

"The Hulk?" Stash shrugs. "That works too."

"Boss!" Sparky waves his hand around to get Rock's attention. "You should go as Darth Vader." He points wildly in Teller's direction, in case we're not all clear on why that's an excellent choice for Rock.

"Only if Charlotte goes in a Princess Leia bikini," Stash adds under his breath.

"You're fucking begging me to beat your ass," Teller shoots back.

"Nah, she's housing twins," Ravage says with a nod that suggests he thinks he's being helpful. "I don't think you'd be able to find a bikini—"

"Are you itching to breathe through a tube for Halloween, brother?" Murphy punches his fist into his open palm. "Because we can make that happen *right now*."

"I just meant—"

"For fuck's sake," Dex snaps, cutting Ravage's explanation off. "When you're standing in a hole, stop fucking digging, Rav."

"The deeper you dig, the more painful your beating's gonna be, brother," Sparky says with a solemn nod.

I shift my gaze to Rock, who has one hand to his temple,

head bowed. Then I notice his shoulders shaking. "All right, enough." He barely conceals his laughter. "I think Hope's planning to go as Sandy—"

I burst out laughing. "From Grease? That's...perfect. Truly. Wait, good girl Sandy or bad girl Sandy? You know what, it doesn't matter. Perfect either way."

Rock glares at me.

"I mean," Z draws the words out slowly, sits back and rubs a sarcastic hand over his hairless chin. "You're already halfway to a Danny Zuko costume with the way you dress, Rock."

"Yeah, but you're the one sporting the late-seventies John Travolta hair," Rooster points out. "Prez," he adds in a semi-respectful tone.

Z runs his hands over his head. "I do not."

"This is fun and whatnot," Grinder says in his least amused grumble. "Everyone's endless knowledge of useless movie trivia is impressive, but can we move things along?"

"Food," Murphy says to Ravage. "You got that all sorted?"

"Of course you're worried about the menu," Ravage mutters.

"Just for that, I'm not gonna try to stop Teller when he kicks your ass after church," Murphy says, sitting back with a smirk.

"As if you would've tried hard," Ravage says.

Everyone actually laughs at that.

"Facts," Murphy mutters.

"Food?" Rock prompts, trying to redirect the conversation.

"A suggestion." I lift one finger in the air to get everyone's attention. "You guys don't need to be hyped up on sugar. Maybe—"

"*Pleeeease* don't give Brother Buzzkill another reason to lecture us on the evils of processed sugar," Sparky moans.

"Why you gotta suck the joy out of everything, Wrath?" Stash asks.

I flick my gaze to the ceiling. These assholes never want to benefit from my wisdom. That's fine. I may be older than the stoner twins but I could still run circles around Sparky while dragging Stash behind me like a trophy buck I shot on opening day of deer season.

"Swan helped us hire someone," Rav says. "To cater."

"Jesus, doesn't that poor girl have enough to do?" Dex asks.

"That's why she helped me find someone to *hire*," Stash says in his best "duh" tone.

"Sounds like we're all good, then." Rock slaps his palm against the table.

"I don't know, Prez." I cast a serious look Rock's way. "This could either be a great time or one hell of a clusterfuck."

CHAPTER TWO

Shelby

ONE WEEK UNTIL HALLOWEEN...

"Why is there a skeleton riding a flamingo like he's a rodeo champion in my front yard?" I pop my hands on my hips and stare Jiggy down, waiting for my answer. This can only be his doing.

Of course, Jigsaw isn't fussed by my interrogation. Nope. Not one bit. He grins at me from my front porch. "What's wrong, songbird? I thought it was an adorable representation of both of your personalities." He rubs his hands in the air like he's molding Lord knows what out of clay.

Behind me, Logan groans and curls his arm around my shoulders.

I flick my gaze toward the tower of bones straddling what seems to be a giant flamingo pool float wearing a witch's hat. "Wait a dang second." I screw my face into a scowl as I try to swallow my laughter. "You tryin' to say that's Rooster ridin' *me?*"

Jigsaw blinks and sputters. "Your man sanctioned it." He jumps off the porch, landing on the grass with a dull thud, and points an accusatory finger Logan's way. "Back me up, brother."

"You said *some* Halloween decorations," Logan counters. "Not this skeleton humping a flamingo monstrosity."

Jigsaw giggles at *humping*. "That's what it looks like, huh?" He squints at the decorations. "I see it now."

"Jesus," Logan grumbles.

I sigh and glance at the decorations again. It's tacky as all get-out but kind of funny, too. It's not like we got lotsa neighbors who'll give a damn anyway. "It's pretty dang clever, Jiggy. And certainly unique."

Jiggy's mouth curls into a smug grin.

"Don't encourage him," Logan protests.

"Songbird-approved." Jiggy slaps Logan's shoulder and jogs into the yard. "Wait until you see the rest of it!"

I peer up at Logan. "There's more?" I whisper.

"I told you not to encourage him."

I give Logan a closer inspection. Blue and gray plaid flannel shirt with the sleeves rolled up just enough to provide an enticing view of his forearms. Dang, my man wears plaid well. I never get tired of looking at him.

"You're looking mighty fine there, Logan." Pressing one hand against his chest, I lean up on tiptoe and kiss his cheek. Bristly beard tickles my lips and I kiss him again. "I think my favorite thing about moving to New York is seeing you in all those flannels you like to wear in the fall."

He grins and slides his arms around my waist, lifting me

higher to plant a longer kiss on my lips. "You're now *my* favorite thing about New York."

"Cock-a-doodle-dooooo!" Jigsaw shouts from outside.

"That's like his mating call for you, isn't it?" I tease.

Logan growls a few curses and sets me down. "Only mating going on around here is you and me."

I wave my hand at him. "You know what I mean."

"Let me go see what he wants. Otherwise, he'll keep on yodeling out there."

I busy myself putting away the few things I picked up at the store. All the different kinds of seltzer available has been another bonus about moving to New York.

Outside, the loud drone of the mail truck zips up, slows, takes off. A few seconds later, the front door bangs open.

"Mail call!" Logan announces. He swaggers in, grinnin' like the cocky critter he got his road name from. In his hands, he's carrying a short stack of envelopes and a small brown box.

"Anythin' good?" I ask.

"Hell yeah." He sets the envelopes—probably bills—on the counter and holds out the box. "I've been waiting for this one. Your Halloween present a few days early."

"It's for me?" Dang it. He got me a Halloween present? Why didn't I think of anything better than a naughty fairy costume for his personal enjoyment?

"Actually, hold on." He pulls a knife out of his pocket and neatly slices through the seal on the box, then hands it to me.

"Thanks." I flip the lid open and strings of holographic

paper flutter to the floor. "Ooops." I lean over to scoop up the rogue packing material, crunching it in my hand. A black velvet pouch is nestled in the center of all the sparkly paper. "What is it?"

"Open." Logan's keen eyes focus on the box as if he's just as excited to see what it is as I am.

Everything looks so pretty, I hate to disturb it, but I carefully lift the silky-soft pouch. It's heavy and neatly cinched together. My fingers detect a rectangular box inside the fabric. Excitement flutters in my belly. Is it a new deck of Tarot cards?

"Oh my goodness," I whisper, setting everything on the counter and unlacing the pouch.

Yup, it's cards. I pull out the sleek, matte black box. Under my fingertips it's smooth and feathery. *Luna Tarot* is embossed in thick, glossy letters on the top.

Gripping the box, I carefully pry it open. A chunky black booklet is nestled on top of a deck of cards wrapped in clear plastic. "It's so pretty. I almost don't want to open it and wreck 'em."

"They're cards. You're supposed to use them," Logan says.

Using my thumbnail, I slice through the thin, crinkly plastic and unwrap the deck. The cards flow into my hands like silk. The backs are made of the same smooth, buttery texture as the box but with raised glossy bumps. I squint and realize a star and galaxy pattern covers the backs of the cards. "They're so pretty." Of all the Tarot decks I've looked at, I've never seen any like these.

Logan's big, warm hand closes around mine. "The galaxy print reminded me of laying out under the stars with you," he says in a quiet voice full of the warmth of a fond memory.

Love and emotion tie my throat in knots. "They're beautiful. I love 'em."

He leans down and presses a kiss to my forehead. "You really like them?"

"Yes." My lips curve up. "In fact, I think they'll go nicely with the costume I'm planning to wear to the club's Halloween party."

One corner of his mouth twitches downward, like maybe he's disappointed? I glance at the cards again. They're fancy. Beautiful little pieces of artwork. Probably expensive. Too nice to take to a party where they could get easily damaged.

I shuffle through the deck again. "Or maybe not. They're too pretty to risk ruining at one of the club's wild parties. I have an old deck I'll bring."

Relief seems to lift his expression. "Does that mean I finally find out what you're going to dress up as for Halloween?"

I hold up the cards, fanning them into a pretty half-circle. "A fortune teller, of course."

Rooster

"Fortune teller, huh? What's my fortune?" I ask Shelby.

She leans up and hugs me. "Lots and lots of kissin' from your fiancée in your immediate *and* distant future."

"I'll take it." I lean down and rub my nose against hers. Her lips slide against mine, soft and feathery.

"Rooster! The fuck!?" Jiggy yells.

"Sheesh." Shelby shakes her head. "Better go. I don't want him accidentally hangin' himself from a dang tree while puttin' up those Halloween lights."

"He's not that fucking dumb." I think better of it and add, "I hope."

She laughs and pats my stomach. "I'm gonna call my momma and tell her about my pretty new cards, then start dinner. You see the size of that box he's got out there? You're gonna work up an appetite."

"Tell Lynn I said hi."

"Will do."

Outside, Jiggy is indeed wrapped up in a ball of tangled string lights. "Good thing I came out here." I gesture to the lights. "Shelby was afraid you might hang yourself with them, but I told her, 'nah, he can't possibly be that stupid.'"

"Joke's on you, motherclucker." He slips his arm out of one coil of lights and holds up what looks like a black plastic spear. "They're solar lights. I'm staking them in the ground not hanging them in the air."

"You gotta wrap 'em around something, no?"

"Yeah, but not my neck."

"Is it my imagination or do you get more annoying every year."

"Definitely your imagination." He smirks and shoves the plastic stake into another flat plastic piece.

An hour later, the maple trees in the front yard each have

either an orange or purple strand of lights wrapped around its base. It's a little sloppy but the lights are a pain in the ass to work with, so I'm not doing it again.

"What's next?" I ask.

"Some lights on the porch railing," he says, as if it should be obvious.

He stops to check his phone and grins. Not his usual demented smile designed to make people piss their pants. The genuine one he reserves for those he trusts and actually gives a shit about. It's the only reason I don't hassle him for fucking around on his phone instead of helping me finish the stupid decorations he insisted on scattering around my front yard.

"It's Jezzie," he says, correctly recognizing my annoyance that he's on his phone. He knows I'd never hassle him for talking to his little sister.

"What's she up to?" The girl's been through a lot, and I like hearing that she's doing well.

He turns the screen my way. "Halloween costumes. She's embracing her demonic, witchy side," he says with all the pride of a papa bear serial killer.

Under the heavy skeleton-witch makeup, the woman on the screen bears a vague resemblance to the girl I remember.

"She do that herself?" I ask.

Jiggy nods and takes his phone back, tapping out a reply. "She's so good with all that shit."

"Am I the only one who doesn't give a crap about Halloween?"

"No. Rock, Wrath, Teller, Grinder, and the other members of Dad alley were equally *un*enthused."

"That's not true. Grinder seemed interested...well, as interested as he gets in anything besides Serena."

Jiggy chuckles. "Those two warm my cold, black heart." He slides his hand in front of his face. "On the surface, they don't seem like they belong together but they're perfect for each other."

"You feeling okay?" I make a show of pressing the back of my hand to his forehead.

"What?" He shrugs and slaps my hand away. "They've both had it rough, so what if I want to see them happy?"

Now I feel like a jackass. "Nah, you're right."

"Well, fuck me sideways." He shoves his hands in his pockets and pulls out an imaginary notepad and pen. "Hang on, let me jot this down. 'Dear diary, today Rooster admitted I'm right about something.'"

"Hilarious." I stare at him. "You planning to finish this project or fuck around all day?"

He taps his chin like a jackass contemplating the meaning of life. "Are you sure you're about to turn thirty and not fifty?"

"Keep digging that grave, brother." I toss a bundle of outdoor extension cords at his midsection. "I'm gonna shove you in it."

"Yeah, yeah." His gaze slides toward the house. "Tell me the truth, did Shelby like it?"

"Once she got over the shock." I glance at the centerpiece of this Halloween wonderland—the ten-foot skeleton riding the flamingo. "It's pretty cool, brother. Thanks for thinking of it." It sure as fuck would never have occurred to me to do this to my lawn.

"Oh! She's going to love these." He yanks out a string of lights with little dancing skeletons dangling from them. "They're for inside, though."

"You're welcome to hang them in your place."

He pulls out his phone again, checks the message, then stares into space for a second.

"You all right?" I ask.

"Yeah. Jezzie says she wants to maybe move to New York and finish school up here."

"That'd be good. Easier to keep an eye on her. Fuck knows there are plenty of colleges in and around Empire."

"I'd like having her closer," he mutters. "I think."

He finishes another text and puts his phone away. "I'll just need to keep the single brothers and the support club away from her, that's all."

I choke on a laugh. "Cool story. Good luck with that."

CHAPTER THREE
Zero

HALLOWEEN MORNING...

Lilly's brother Alex has to be one of my least favorite people. I can endure anything for a couple of minutes, though. Worst-case scenario—we're at his house for a couple of hours. No, worst-case would be I punch him in the mouth in front of Lilly and Chance. My love for my family pulses around me like a living, breathing shadow of hostility, always prepared to protect them at any cost.

Focus on the positive. Alex is good to my son. Chance loves his Uncle Alex. According to Lilly, Alex has stopped pestering her about being married to a thug—me. His opinion doesn't bother me one bit. I *am* a thug. One who will murder to protect his family. Alex can't be bothered to open his mouth to stick up for his sister around their parents. My interest in his opinion rests somewhere around zero percent.

I swallow all those thoughts down for Chance's sake.

He's too little for ugly family history lessons. Today's supposed to be about fun.

"He knows we're on the way, right?" I ask, glancing over at Lilly.

She tucks her phone in her purse. "He said any time after ten but I just sent him a text to let him know we'll be there in half an hour."

"Good." Last thing I want to do is wake the grouchy asshole up.

"Thank you for this." Lilly rests her hand on my thigh. "I know it's the last thing you feel like doing."

I can think of a few other activities that rate lower than this—digging a grave, cleaning dog vomit out of the carpet, and dissolving a body in acid all come to mind. That probably won't give Lilly the warm fuzzies, though. Keeping one hand on the steering wheel, I rest the other over hers. "Too bad we didn't bring Grace, so Alex could get the full effect of their costumes."

"Grace? Where?" Chance asks from the back seat.

One-track mind my son has.

"We'll see her at Uncle Wrath's place a little later, buddy," I tell him.

In the rearview, I catch his lips pinching into a pout as he stares out the window.

Lilly turns in her seat. "You want to show Uncle Alex your costume, right?"

"Yes!" Chance is all smiles now.

Yup, there's that twinge in my chest again. Reminding me that I'll do anything to make my kid happy.

Even hang out with Alex for a few hours.

Lilly

"Do you remember what to say?" I ask Chance as we approach the front door of my brother's house.

Chance squints up at me. "Click o' tweet."

"Trick or treat," I say slowly.

Behind us, Z chuckles.

Instead of knocking, Chance throws his bright green pumpkin-shaped bucket against the door.

"Easy, buddy." Z pulls the bucket away from the door while I give it a more proper knock.

Chance shoots both of us a toothy little grin.

The door opens and Alex flashes a tight smile at me. Ignoring Z completely, he leans down and scoops Chance into his arms. "Happy Halloween, little man."

"Rawr!"

"Come in, come in." Alex steps aside and motions us forward. He closes the door behind us, then wraps me in a quick embrace. A flowery scent clings to his sweater, tickling my nose.

"Hey, Z." My brother offers Z a quick handshake.

"Trick or treat!" Chance shouts, waving his bucket around. "Where's my candy?"

"Chance," Z warns.

Alex scratches his head like he has no idea what my son's talking about. "Candy? First, you have to show me your costume. What are you?"

"A wolf-mer-jack." Chance pulls a tiny plastic ax out of his pumpkin bucket and shakes the fuzzy ears on his head.

Alex tosses me a skeptical look and I shrug. "He wanted to be a big, bad wolf *and* a lumberjack."

"Grace is red hood," Chance adds.

"Hope's daughter," I remind Alex in case he doesn't remember who Grace is. "She's going to be Little Red Riding Hood."

"Ah, I get it." Alex nods. "Cute."

"Hey." A softer, feminine voice greets us.

I look past my brother, into the living room.

Sophie.

What the hell?

I haven't seen my ex-best friend in...I try to do the math. Four years? Five? A large chunk of the past few years of my life remains clouded. Pieces of my history I've put behind me and prefer not to examine too closely.

Sadness weighs on my heart. We were the best of friends growing up. Every crazy adventure we went on together. All the times we got into trouble with our parents for not being "good girls." The boys we cried over in high school. The road trips when we got our licenses. Every moment comes rushing back to me.

With those memories comes a truth that's hard to admit to myself. I didn't like the person I was back then. The acting out was a reaction to overly strict, cruel parents who made me feel worthless. We bonded over the pain of not quite fitting into our families.

Alex moves closer to Sophie and takes her hand.

My stomach rolls. Obviously, she didn't stop by for a candy bar. They're...something.

Together.

When we were kids, Sophie had a crush on Alex. She spent a lot of time trying to capture his attention. Supposedly they had a fling in college but since they wanted two very different things in life, it didn't last.

Priorities change. I know that better than anyone.

I slip my hand into Z's, and he gives it a reassuring squeeze. I certainly never planned to find myself wildly in love with and married to a biker.

Alex clears his throat. "I wanted to tell you. But not over the phone," he begins.

So you thought ambushing me was a good idea?

I force what I hope looks like a genuine smile. "Tell me what?"

Sophie stares up at my brother and he flashes an affectionate smile at her. "We've been seeing each other for a while," Sophie finally says.

Seeing each other? It's more than that. She's clearly comfortable enough in my brother's house to run around in nothing but one of his over-sized T-shirts.

Don't be catty.

"That's great. I'm so happy for you guys." *Dammit, Lilly. Can't you sound more sincere than that?*

Sophie's face breaks into a smile and she steps forward to embrace me. "Thank you," she whispers against my hair.

My resistance melts and I return the hug. "It's good to see you."

She pulls away, searching my face. "You too. It's been a while."

"It has."

Moving away from me, she rakes her gaze over my husband. "Z, you made an honest woman out of my girl after all."

He gives her a tight smile. "How've you been, Sophie?"

"Good. Better." She shrugs and squats down to say hello to Chance.

He eyes her warily.

"I'm your Aunt Sophie." She holds out her hand for him.

My son screws his face into a scowl and peers up at me.

I'm with you, kiddo. Aunt Sophie seems a bit presumptuous.

If we were still friends, I probably wouldn't think twice about it. Hell, if she marries Alex, I won't have a choice. I smile and nod at him.

He lets her shake his hand, then pulls away and waves his pumpkin bucket at Alex. "Candy?"

The adults burst into laughter, which eases the tension that crept over us.

"Yeah, I got you, champ." Alex sweeps his hand toward the kitchen. "Follow me."

Sophie's gaze ping-pongs between Z and me. "Can we talk for a second?" she asks me.

Z lifts his chin. "Go ahead, I'm gonna see if Alex has some extra candy for me." He leans in and kisses my cheek.

Sophie tilts her head toward the sliding glass door leading

to the stone patio Alex built a few summers ago. She flips the tricky latch on the door with ease.

Someone's been spending a lot of time here.

Outside, she tilts her head back and closes her eyes, inhaling the cool, crisp fall air. The scent of wet leaves hangs heavy around us. Alex's yard is usually pristine, but it looks like he's fallen behind on yard maintenance this year.

I wait, quietly, curious to hear what she has to say.

"I hope you're not mad about us." She gestures toward the house.

"Not at all," I answer, honestly. Off-balance and confused, yes. Mad, no. "Just a little surprised."

"Alex was really there for me," she says, hesitating on every other word. "I'm completely sober now. Almost a year."

"That's great." I'm genuinely happy for her but still unsure of what she expects from me. An apology forms on my tongue but I bite it back. Sorry for what? Not holding her hand through who knows how many trips to rehab? When she couldn't even say one supportive thing when I—

No.

I keep my mouth shut and wait.

She gestures toward the diamond on my left hand. "Congratulations." A hesitant smile flickers over her lips. "Chance is adorable. He looks exactly like Z. Alex showed me pictures but it's even more obvious seeing them together in person."

Unsure if that's some backhanded way of asking if I ever questioned Chance's paternity, I only hum a noise of agreement.

"How's Hope?" she asks. "You said she has a daughter?"

"She's good."

"She's still with Rock?"

I grind my teeth, annoyed she'd even ask. "They're very happy together." Hope wouldn't appreciate me telling Sophie anything about her marriage, so I keep it to the bare minimum.

"That's good." The corners of her mouth turn down. "I guess you two are pretty tight now, huh?"

"I guess."

She bites her lip and shifts her gaze to the patio door. "Look, whatever I did when I was drinking, I don't... remember." She touches her fingers to her forehead lightly. "Alex said you were living in California for a while? I...I don't remember. I'm sorry, though."

I blow out a long breath. Should I be happy she has no memory of the conversation that, in my mind, ended our friendship? Probably. If she doesn't remember, that means she couldn't have told my brother. But I'm not quite sure I believe her when she says she has no memory of it.

Senator Kelly's long dead. I don't ever want Sophie to put the pieces together and think Z had something to do with the murder. And I really don't want my brother to suspect anything.

I paste on a bigger smile. "I understand. Apology accepted." In a softer voice, I add, "You look good. I'm happy for you."

She lets out a relieved breath. "Thank you. I don't want there to be weirdness, you know, between us."

"No weirdness," I confirm, then laugh. "Well, besides the idea *anyone* would want to date my brother."

She blinks, then realizes I'm kidding and laughs with me. "He's a force of nature."

It certainly seems Alex has been supportive of Sophie. "You could say that."

"So." She swings her arms at her sides like she's shaking off the awkwardness. "Are you guys staying?"

"Can't. I told Alex, we have something in Empire that starts in a little bit."

"Club stuff?" She raises her eyebrows.

I open my mouth to explain it's a charity event, then think better of it. What if she wants to tag along? I'm not ready for that. "Yes," I say, hoping that squelches any desire to attend.

She nods. "I think we're staying in, watching horror movies, and handing out candy." A soft smile flickers over her mouth as if she's content with a quiet night on what used to be her favorite party holiday. The thought makes me...happy. Maybe she really has changed.

"Sounds perfect. We did that last weekend to get in the Halloween spirit."

We chat for a few more minutes. Nothing of significance. It's nice to catch up and let go of some of the hurt and anger I'd been holding onto.

The sliding glass door rumbles open and Alex steps out. "Everything okay?"

What'd he think we were going to do, have a catfight on the lawn?

"Great!" Sophie's voice is full of a bit more cheer than necessary.

"All good," I agree.

"I need to run inside." Sophie squeezes Alex's arm on her way in the door.

My brother slides the door closed and shoves his hands in his pockets. Guilt crawls over his face. "I didn't mean to ambush you but I'm glad you finally know."

"You could've mentioned it." I lean in and lightly punch his arm.

"Hey, your other friend got married," he chuckles.

I stare at him, surprised he'd say something so stupid. "You better never say that to Sophie," I warn.

I may have reservations about having Sophie back in *my* life, but that doesn't mean I want my brother to treat her like she's some second runner-up in the Alex's affection contest.

"I'm kidding, Lilly." He shakes his head. "You know we... it's always been Sophie."

No, I didn't know that. "Well, I'm happy for both of you."

"Thanks." He stares at the ground for a few seconds. Either he's about to say something profound or he's thinking about digging up the patio stones and evening them out. Hard to tell with Alex. "I was a bit of an asshole to you about Z, so I guess I was worried you'd return the favor."

"Oh, Alex, I'm not that petty." I mean it as a joke, but it comes out a little harsh.

He blows out a breath. "I'm bringing her to Mom and Dad's Sunday. I'd love if you were there too."

That's a hell-fucking-no. "I'll check and see if we're able to."

His gaze slides to the door. "Z doesn't have to come if he's busy."

"That's never happening." In a flash, I see how that dinner would go. Alex would use me to protect Sophie from their scrutiny and disapproval. I'd have the honor of being lectured and called names all night.

Been there. Done that.

"Well, let me know."

We step back inside. Chance is sprawled out on the couch with his head in Z's lap.

"Sugar crash?" I ask Z.

"Think so," he whispers. "I'll carry him out. He'll probably wake up by the time we get there."

After a few rounds of goodbyes, we head to Z's truck. Relief washes over me as we turn onto the Northway, headed for Wrath's gym.

"You okay?" Z asks.

"Sorry I left you with Alex. Did he behave?"

"Yeah, he was fine. Mostly talked to Chance. I asked him a few tree removal questions."

"Oh, that probably made his day." For someone who claims to enjoy being seen as a "scary biker," Z's awfully adept at socializing in any situation.

"Do you want to talk about Sophie?" he asks.

"It was quite a shock."

"A heads-up from your brother would've been nice," he grumbles, flicking on his blinker to pass a slow Cadillac.

"If they're happy, I'm happy for them." I bite my lip, considering how to put my thoughts into words. No one has ever understood or accepted me the way Z does, so I shouldn't be afraid to voice my feelings.

"We were so close growing up," I start. "But I'm in such a different place in my life now." For some stupid reason my eyes and the back of my throat sting. "I realize a lot of those memories aren't really happy ones."

Z rests his hand over mine. "Some people come into your life for a short amount of time, and some for a lifetime. Friends—even good ones—can grow apart and that's okay," he says gently.

"She hurt me when I was in a bad place," I say in a stronger voice. "I was always there for her when she was in a jam. The one time I really needed her, she blew me off." I grab my water bottle and take a quick sip. "As much as it stung, I don't think it was intentional. But I also don't think it was one hundred percent the alcohol's fault."

"People can be addicts and shitty humans at the same time," he says. "One doesn't have to be the cause of the other."

I understand Z's firm feelings on this issue. "I want to be compassionate. People are capable of change and growth. But I also don't have the space in my life for the drama and negativity she used to bring."

"Lilly, you're one of the most compassionate people I know." He squeezes my hand. "Even though you *were* shocked to see her, you *were* kind." His full lips twist into a wry smirk. "You were a lot nicer about Alex dating her than he was about you and me being together."

Laughter tickles the back of my throat. "True." I let out a sigh. "Alex mentioned that too. Almost sounded like an apology."

He grunts a doubtful sound.

"He tried to rope me into dinner at my parents Sunday. He's bringing Sophie and probably wants to use me as a buffer."

His hands tighten on the steering wheel. "We can go if you want to."

His offer means more than I can express. "I told him no."

"Sounds like she's going to be in your life now," Z says.

What is that future going to look like? Christmas dinners with Sophie and my brother?

Oh shit. As far as I know, Hope and Sophie never mended their friendship. How's Hope going to feel about me spending time with Sophie? Hope's my club sister. And truthfully, she's been a better friend to me than Sophie ever was. She's always there for me when I need anything. She treats Chance like her own and he adores his Auntie Hope.

"What am I going to say to Hope?" I blurt out.

"That girl doesn't have a spiteful bone in her body," he answers with calm certainty. "Hope's not going to hold it against you if you hang out with Sophie every now and then." He snorts. "Knowing her, she'll find it romantic that Alex and Sophie are together."

"You're probably right."

Even so, worry eats at me for the rest of the drive.

CHAPTER FOUR

Hope

"I'm back," Rock shouts.

"Up here!" I check my costume in the mirror one more time.

"Daddy!" Grace yelps.

"Go get your cape to show Daddy," I say to Grace. She nods enthusiastically and scurries to her room.

Rock unlatches the baby gate at the top of the stairs and steps into our room a few seconds later. Something rustles behind his back. "Almost ready?"

"Yup."

He pulls a thick bouquet of purple and orange roses wrapped in black and purple paper from behind his back. "Happy Halloween, baby doll."

"Oh!" I gasp and hurry closer, gently taking the flowers from him. "These are beautiful. Where'd you find them?"

He half-shrugs. "A small thank you for putting up with all of this club stuff today."

"I'm looking forward to it." I step back and spin for him to check out my costume. "I'm going to the Furious party like this. Then I'll change into my other costume at the clubhouse."

"You're the sexiest granny I've ever laid eyes on." Rock runs his gaze over my kid-appropriate costume for the afternoon.

I tug at the red dress and white apron and dip in a half-curtsy. "A little preview of what's to come a few decades from now, Mr. President."

Laughter flickers over his lips and he tugs on my white bonnet. "Looking forward to it."

I stick my nose in the roses, inhaling their rich scent. "I really love these. Thank you."

"Momma!" Grace toddles into our bedroom, dragging her little red velvet cape behind her.

Rock squats to her level and reaches for the cape. Grace yanks it out of his grasp.

"Do you want to wear it now or when we get to the party?" he asks her.

She frowns at the cape, then up at me.

"You can hold it," I assure her.

She hugs the cape to her chest, then eyes my roses, reaching for them with tiny fingers.

Rock picks her up, bouncing her gently in his arms until she squees with delight.

"Is this the dress?" he asks me, running his fingers over the red and black checked flannel. He brings her closer and I hold out the flowers for Grace to inspect.

"I was going for warmth over authenticity," I explain. "Chance's shirt matches. They'll be so cute together." I set the roses on the bed so I can fix the frilly lace at the collar of Grace's dress and tug one ankle of her black leggings into place. "Where are your socks?" I ask her.

She squirms until Rock sets her down, then runs out of our room.

Laughing, Rock walks over to the doorway to watch her. A few seconds later, Grace returns, dragging her cape with one hand and clutching the socks in her other, arm raised triumphantly.

"Good job." Rock picks her up again and she grins at me over his shoulder.

I hold out my hand and she plops the socks against my palm. "We'll put them on downstairs."

"Okay!" she chirps.

"Go ahead, Rock." I turn, searching for my overnight bag. "I want to make sure I have everything. Grace's stuff is all packed downstairs."

I swear it feels like we're going away for a week rather than an overnight stay at the Empire clubhouse.

"I'm going to put these in water," Rock says, grabbing the flowers.

"Thank you."

I shoot a text to Trinity asking if she needs me to bring a curling iron to the clubhouse. When I don't get a response right away, I grab one and shove it into an outside pocket of my backpack—just in case.

Downstairs, Rock's at the kitchen counter, scowling at his

41

phone. The flowers are high on the counter where Grace can't reach them, in a purple vase. I stop to rub the petals between my fingers, admiring the deep purples and oranges.

I set our bags on the bench by the front door. Grace is sitting on her cape in the middle of the living room floor, playing with the little stuffed doll Charlotte gave her yesterday.

Rock's furiously tapping out a text to someone.

"Everything okay?" I ask.

"No. Knucklehead thinks he doesn't have to go to the party tonight." He curses under his breath. "I don't know what part of *everyone needs to be there* was so hard for him to understand."

I bite the inside of my cheek so I don't laugh. Even with their relationship out in the open, Rock and Teller continue to butt heads with each other from time to time. While I still think it's normal behavior as they get adjusted to their new roles, it drives Rock nuts. They're both headstrong men. Gee, what are the odds they'd clash once in a while? They're alike in so many ways, especially in the stubbornness department.

"Maybe he's worried about Charlotte," I suggest.

He stares at the ceiling for a few seconds. "I understand that, but I can't order everyone else to be there and then give him a pass. Bricks also expressed some annoyance about it, yesterday. If I had to tell him to suck it up, then the same has to go for Marcel, too."

"I understand." I run my tongue over my bottom lip, considering if I should even offer this suggestion. "Have you thought about having Wrath be the one to deal with Teller in an MC capacity? He's good at laying down the law. Then you two can just work on your father-son relationship." *And if Teller gives him lip, Wrath will snap him like a twig.* I don't say that part out loud, though.

"Wrath might break his neck if he throws attitude at him." Rock's mouth curves into a feral grin. "But yeah, discipline is supposed to be his role, anyway."

I duck my head and laugh. "At least until Teller works through this 'pushing-Dad's-buttons' phase he's going through."

"You think that's what it is?" he asks.

"Some of it, yes. I think he's also worried about Charlotte and the babies. First-time dad stress." I pause and try to word this next part carefully. "I understand you're trying not to show favoritism toward him now that the club knows he's your son, but don't go too far the other way and be too hard on him, either."

"Too hard on him," he repeats in a grudging tone.

"And don't forget he's babysitting for us tonight," I remind him.

"I know. That's why I said he doesn't have to stay at the party too long. But I need him to show his face." Rock holds up his phone in his fist. "Now he's saying he 'feels like skipping it.' As if it was optional. Fucker."

"Oh, well." Gosh, Teller must be feeling suicidal tonight. "Tell him 'tough shit.' *Skipping it* isn't an option."

"That's what I said." He shoves his phone in his pocket. "Let's stop by his place on our way to Furious."

"Only if you promise not to choke him."

"Baby doll, I can promise you a lot of things." He steps in front of me and rests his hands on my hips, pulling me closer. "That's not one of them."

Rock

Hope's calm, rational presence is probably the only thing stopping me from throttling my son today.

"You have to at least stop by," I warn Marcel. I swear if he gives me one more dickish smirk...

"I'm going to be busy here." He holds out his arms. "With all my little guests."

A spot behind my right eye throbs. Hope was right about that button-pushing thing.

Our gazes stray to the small maze Marcel and Carter built for the kids out of hay bales. Alexa and Grace had spent most of yesterday running through it. And screaming bloody murder the few times they'd run into a dead end. Today, Grace is more interested in grabbing fistfuls of hay and tossing them in the air. Hope runs after her, thwarting Grace's attempts to dismantle the whole thing.

"It's fine, Hope," Marcel calls out.

Hope gives up and tosses her own handful of hay.

Marcel chuckles and turns to face me again.

I'm not laughing.

"When Heidi and Murphy get here later, I expect you to take your ass down to Empire and visit that fucking clubhouse," I say.

"I've already seen it."

What's so hard for him to understand about this? Hope got it immediately. Maybe I should strip Marcel's patch and give it to my wife. "You heard me tell *everyone* they need to be there."

He opens his mouth, probably to protest some more, but I cut him off.

"I can't give you special treatment." I cock my head and drill him with a hard stare. "You get that, right? The club accepted the news that you're my son with no issue, but I can't give them the impression that I play favorites."

He seems to consider that for a second or two. "I have a pregnant wife I don't want to leave." He waves his hand toward the house.

Guilt pokes at me but I remain firm. "So does Grinder. Serena's going with him. Charlotte can go with you."

His thoughtful expression shifts into a glare. "Don't tell me how to handle my wife."

I work my jaw from side to side. He seems committed to being deliberately obtuse today.

"We don't get trick-or-treaters." He waves his hand toward the house. "But I still worry someone might try to fuck with the place if Charlotte's here by herself."

"But she won't be alone. Go early. Show your face around, then come home. That's all I'm asking of you."

"Fuck." He runs his hand over the back of his neck. "Fine. I'm not wearing a fucking costume, though."

Is that my last thread of patience snapping? "No one asked you to."

His insolent mouth slides into a smirk. "What are *you* going as?"

"An MC president with a mouthy son he'd like to smack around."

"How creative." He rolls his eyes. "You'll be unrecognizable."

As the intensity of our conversation dies down, Charlotte sneaks up behind Marcel and wraps her arms around his waist, pressing her cheek against his back. "Are you giving your father lip?" she asks in a teasing voice.

"Yes," I answer at the same time Marcel answers, "No."

Charlotte's red lips curl into a knowing smile. Thank Buddha this woman is—*for some reason*—charmed by all of my son's irritating qualities.

"I was explaining to *my president*," Marcel drags out the words, "that I have better things to do tonight than watch Ravage get his dick sucked by every muffler bunny in the tri-state area?"

Charlotte wrinkles her nose. "*Every* bunny? Surely some of them have higher standards?"

I snort and focus my attention on her. "You doing all right, Charlotte?"

She nods and squeezes Marcel one last time before releasing him and rubbing her hand over her belly. "I feel good, actually. I even have my costume picked out for tonight."

Marcel's eyes widen and he turns toward her. "You do?"

"Yup. Heidi came up with it. Green dress." She rubs her

stomach again. "I'm going to attach two light green circles on my belly and go as 'peas in a pod.'"

Much-needed laughter bursts out of me. "Nice."

"You need us to stop by the new clubhouse, right?" Charlotte asks. "I'm looking forward to getting out of the house for at least a few minutes."

I poke Marcel's chest. "You should be ashamed of yourself. Trying to use your wife to get out of tonight."

Charlotte's jaw drops and she turns toward Marcel. "What? Why? You know I want to go and see everyone."

Have fun with that, knucklehead.

Serves him right for being such a pain in my ass.

Satisfied Charlotte will chew him out, I stalk over to the maze and surprise Grace by scooping her into my arms and kissing her cheek.

"You're not going to give me trouble when you're older, are you?" I murmur against her ear.

"Nooooo, Da-da." She wraps her arms around my neck and hugs tight enough to squeeze most of my irritation away.

"All good?" Hope asks quietly, stepping up behind Grace and resting a hand on her back.

"We came to an understanding."

The corners of her mouth curl. "I'm sure." She flicks her gaze at Teller and Charlotte. "Well, he's still standing and breathing, so that's good."

"Where are your granny glasses, Hope?" Charlotte calls out.

Laughing, Hope squeezes my arm as she leaves to talk to Charlotte.

"Pop-pop!" Alexa shouts about two seconds before she plows into my leg.

Grace wriggles, wanting to get down and play. The girls hold hands and scamper toward the hay bales. Alexa helps Grace climb on top of one and like the mush they've turned me into, I pull out my phone to snap a bunch of photos. *Family time.* Exactly what I need before dealing with more club bullshit later.

Balance. Life's all about balance.

CHAPTER FIVE
Wrath

Good God, what hell did I unleash on my gym? We're not even open yet but bikes, trucks, and Trinity's Jeep fill up the parking lot next door. My parking lot is full of a maze of hay bales taller than I am. And a scarecrow. What the fuck? Scarecrows in the middle of Empire. Fucking ridiculous.

I stop and send Trinity a text, letting her know I'm here.

October chill follows me across the parking lot. There's a flash of metal in the sunlight as the door swings open. Trinity rushes out, slamming into me. I curl my arms around her and lift her for a kiss.

"I'm so happy you're here," she whispers against my lips. "Can't wait for you to see everything."

I set her down and hold her at arm's length. "I want to look at you first."

She grabs the sides of her long, white dress and swings it from side to side. Braided gold thread on the sleeves flashes in the sunlight. Her bright blonde hair's a mass of long, spiral curls spilling down her back. She touches her shoulders. "I still have a few pieces to add before the event starts."

I'm struck stupid and can't say a damn word. Fucking Angel. She's turned my nickname for her—Angel—into a reality. Well, *my* version of an angel. "You look perfect as is."

"Thank you." She flutters her lashes. "The costume gets sexier as the night goes on."

Great. Now the last thing I want to do is deal with screaming kids all afternoon.

"I'll just need you to help me put my wings on in a little bit." She taps her shoulders.

"I don't want to put more clothes *on* you. I want to rip everything *off*, Angel Face."

She trails her fingers over my chest, stopping to play with the buttons of my flannel shirt. "If you're good," she purrs, "by the end of the night I'll be wearing nothing *but* the wings."

"Promise?" I should get this in writing.

She wiggles her eyebrows.

That's not exactly confirmation.

The back door swings open again. Jake throws his arms out in a what-the-fuck gesture. "Been waitin' for your big ass all day. What's the hold up?"

"Watch it, you suicidal little ferret." I curl one arm around Trinity, tucking her against my side, and reach out to slap my palm against Jake's cheek. Lightly. Well, lightly for me.

"Ferret?" Jake shouts, pointing to the dumbass brown

ears sticking out of his wild mop of curly brown hair. "They're *lion* ears." He points to Trinity. "She made me wear them."

Laughter rumbles through me and I hug Trinity tighter. My wife's givin' me gifts all day long.

I step through the door and stop in my tracks. While I'd helped Jake and Murphy move things around last night—according to Trinity's strict directions—I steered clear of the decorating. I have to give my talented wife credit—she and Carter turned my gym into a fun but spooky little hellscape for the kids of Empire.

Equipment has been moved and hidden behind black panels to keep our visitors safe. Trinity went with a "dark forest" theme. Carter painted ominous pine trees and stone paths against a midnight blue background on the panels. Goblins and other freaky creatures peek out from behind branches and orange leaves. Ghosts and spiderwebs dangle from above. Small purple lights dot the path our visitors are supposed to take throughout the "forest." As we venture deeper into the maze, spindly black trees with orange pumpkin ornaments appear. Buckets of candy are tucked away in different corners.

"They have to work to find the candy," Trinity says.

"Is someone handing it out?" I ask. "Or is it just a free-for-all?"

She shrugs. "Does it matter? Trust me, I bought more than enough. If anything's left over, I'll bring it to the clubhouse for tonight's party."

"What if some little goblin steals the whole bucket?"

Another shrug. "Then I guess they earned it." A sad expression crosses her face. "I never got to do fun Halloween stuff when I was a kid, so I'm not saying no to any of these kids and ruining their fun."

How can I argue with that? "All right. Maybe we should have Hope draw up a waiver saying if some kid pukes all over his parents' house, they won't sue us?"

She rolls her eyes but laughs, which is what I was after. "You're the owner." She pats my chest, then turns to fix one of the hanging pumpkin ornaments. "I'll leave the legal stuff to you."

"Hey." I grab her hand, tug her backward, and wrap my arms around her. Leaning down, I kiss her cheek and whisper in her ear, "Thank you. This is really...everything you did is amazing."

Her body melts against mine and she tips her head back. "It wasn't me. Bricks added the glow in the dark paint. And Carter's been painting his ass off for two weeks."

"Yeah, but I don't think Scribbles will appreciate a kiss from me." I attack her neck and shoulder, kissing and nibbling loudly until she's squirming and giggling in my arms.

"Maybe not," she gasps, and laughs some more. "But make sure you thank him." Her tone turns more serious. "He's still having a hard time since the toe incident."

"I'll make sure to thank him," I promise.

"You two realize this is a PG event, right?" Jake calls out behind us.

When he's close enough, I wrap an arm around his neck

and choke-hug him to my side. "Thanks for being cool with this."

"Yeah, yeah." He executes a spin move to get away from me and Trinity applauds.

"You'll have to teach me that move at the next class," she says to him.

"You wanna get away from me, Angel Face?" I ask.

"Never."

Jake sticks his index finger down his throat and pretends to gag.

"Keep it up." I reach out and shove him sideways, almost knocking him into one of the black trees. "I'll give you something to choke on."

He squints. "That sounds dirty."

Trinity snort-laughs into her hand.

"And you're not my type," Jake adds.

"How have I let you live all these years?" I ask.

He's saved from answering by the back door opening. Little giggles and Hope's softer voice echo through the otherwise quiet gym.

"Back here, Hope!" Trinity shouts.

I bust up laughing as soon as I see Hope in her granny get-up. "The fuck are you supposed to be, Cinderella?"

"*That* would've been a better costume choice." She tugs her white bonnet into place.

"What are you supposed to be?" Rock asks me. "A feral Sasquatch?"

I scratch my beard. "Aren't all Sasquatches feral?"

"Look at you!" Trinity leans over to check out little Grace's costume.

"Red Riding Hood?" I ask Hope.

She nods.

"Granny. Got it. Why isn't Rock the big, bad wolf?"

"Chance is the wolf," Hope says with an eye roll, as if that's something I should've known.

"When are they getting here?" Trinity checks her phone. "Heidi and Alexa are almost here." She smiles at Grace. "We need all our little monsters here so the mash can begin."

CHAPTER SIX

Hope

IT'S BEEN YEARS SINCE MY DAYS OF WORKING RETAIL, collecting money from strangers. At least my job today is simple and straightforward. Five dollars per family. Cash in an envelope tucked inside my apron. Smile. Admire the costumes.

Trinity said she only needed me for ten minutes. That was half an hour ago.

There's a lull in the line and I step inside Furious to warm up. "Getting chilly out there," I say to Heidi, who's been handing out treats as the kids enter the "haunted forest."

"Do you want to switch?"

I scan the interior but through the purple lights, spider webs, and dark trees, I can't see a thing.

"Uncle Rock's in Wrath's office with the girls," Heidi says, guessing correctly who I'm searching for.

The door whooshes open behind me. Damn. "I better get back to my post."

I turn and smack into Lilly. "You're here! Any chance I can talk you into working the front door?"

Z's standing behind her and he grins down at me.

"Where's Chance?" I ask.

Z lifts his chin. "Out back with Uncle Bricks and the kids."

"Rock's in Wrath's office."

Z and Lilly share a look, a sort of silent communication they've developed. After a second or two, he nods and disappears into Halloweenland.

"I have to talk to you," Lilly whispers, grabbing my arm and tugging me outside.

"I'm supposed to be collecting money," I protest.

Heidi steps in to take my place. "I've got it, Hope. Go ahead."

Lilly practically drags me to the edge of the side parking lot and wedges us in between two trucks. "What's wrong, Lilly?"

"We stopped at my brother's on the way here." She waves her hands toward the building. Something shook Lilly. She's usually so calm.

"Is Alex okay?" I ask. I always liked him. Once upon a time, he supposedly had a crush on me. The one occasion he tried to ask me out, I shot him down.

"Oh, he's ducky." She shakes her head and stares somewhere over my shoulder. "He wasn't alone."

"Really?" I wiggle my eyebrows. "Alex is seeing someone? Good for him."

"Not *someone*." She takes a deep breath and shifts her gaze back to me. "Sophie."

It takes a moment for that to sink in. "Wow. That's, uh, unexpected." I shrug. "Good for them. Didn't you say they hooked up in high school or something? They rekindled their...romance or whatever? That's kind of sweet."

She blows out a breath and relaxes her shoulders. "You're not mad?"

Confused, I frown. "Mad? No. Was it weird for *you*? He's your brother." I know why Sophie and I aren't friends anymore, but even so, I don't wish her ill will or anything. We've both just moved on with our lives and I'm fine with that.

Lilly, on the other hand, has never quite told me what caused the rift in her relationship with Sophie.

"Maybe *mad* wasn't the right word." She bites her lip. "I felt like I was...I don't know, betraying you by being forced to hang out with her."

Forced. Yikes. Lilly's really not taking this well. "She was your friend long before you and I met. It's okay." I nudge my shoulder against hers. "I understand."

"Yeah, but you're like my sister now," she says softly.

"Aw. Come here." I pull her in for a hug. Slowly, she wraps her arms around me. We stand like that for a few minutes and eventually, she seems to relax.

Finally, she pulls away. "Thanks."

"I never asked," I say as tactfully as possible, "why you

two aren't friends anymore? You don't have to tell me if you don't want to," I add quickly.

Her eyes take on a distant look. "I...uh...something shitty happened to me and when I tried to talk to her about it, she blew me off. Kind of blamed *me* for it, actually." She stares at the trees lining the edge of the parking lot. "It stung. I didn't bother calling her again and she didn't reach out either. I know she was still drinking at the time...hell, I'm not even sure she remembers. She says she doesn't." Lilly bites her lip. "No, she remembers, she had this guilty look in her eyes when she apologized." Lilly shakes her head. "I don't know what to think. It's in the past."

"Well, I'm here for you. No matter what you decide to do."

"She asked about you." Lilly quickly shakes her head. "I didn't give her many details. I mentioned Grace to Alex and—"

"Lilly, it's fine. Really."

"Thanks."

I loop my arm through hers. "Come on, let's go check out the maze. It's pretty cool."

Instead of going inside the gym to go out the back door, we walk around the building to where the outdoor maze is set up.

Tall skeletons guard the entrance and loud shrieks pierce the air.

"Yeah, I'm going to pass," Lilly says. "The only kids I want to be around are ours."

Laughing, I nod in agreement and we continue toward the back of the maze.

"What's with the creepy-ass scarecrows?" she whispers.

I frown, staring at the two staked scarecrows. "Weird, there was only one before."

"Part of the decor, I guess."

One of them looks weird, though. Torn, dirty jeans with pieces of hay poking out. A ripped, filthy flannel covers a hay-filled chest. It has a much more human shape than the lifeless, store-bought one next to it.

"Please tell me they didn't hang a prospect from a stick," I whisper to Lilly.

"Prospect or club enemy?" she whispers back. A trail of nervous laughter follows.

"They wouldn't do something so risky with so many people here," I say.

But what if a club enemy dumped a body here?

A cool breeze picks up, stirring the leaves in a circle around us. Soft, crunchy autumn whispers that I usually find comforting.

I search the area and spot Rock by the gym with Z, Grace, and Chance. He nods at me. I lift my hand in a half-hearted wave.

"Hope!" Lilly grabs my arm. "It moved."

"What?" I whirl around and find her tiptoeing closer to the scarecrow.

"Lilly, what are you doing?" I hiss, hurrying to catch up.

We can't be in danger, we're surrounded by people.

"Come closer, little girls," the scarecrow rasps in an eerie voice.

Lilly and I scream and grab each other.

My granny costume should've included a pair of Depends.

CHAPTER SEVEN

Jigsaw

I'm DEFINITELY GOING TO HELL FOR TEASING NOT ONE but *two* presidents' ol' ladies. But I'm committed. The show must continue.

I've been hanging here for at least fifteen minutes waiting to scare the shit out of Rooster.

But it's Hope and Lilly who find me first. This could be fun.

Or get me killed.

"What the hell?" Hope gasps.

I slowly lift my arms over my head and recite a version of the creepy Halloween poem I've used for years.

"Halloween time the dead arise,
Demons will play tricks with your eyes,
Goblins of every shape give chase,
Scream all you want, there's no escape!"

I jump down, landing in front of the girls with a thud.

They let out short, shrill screams.

I point a finger at them and shuffle closer.

The hay in my costume scratches some intimate places but I continue zombie-walking toward them.

"Jigsaw!" Lilly yelps. "Dammit, is that you?"

I cackle with glee and run after them, bowlegged and spilling hay everywhere. Satan help me, I'm trying hard not to covet my president's wife, but Lilly's curves are insane.

A thought I'll take with me to the grave.

I'm close enough to tap their shoulders when Hope stops dead, spins around, and charges me.

Shit, wasn't expecting that.

She yanks the hat off my head and squints up at me. "You nut! Why would you do that to us?"

"Are you looking for a better answer than, it's Halloween?" I hold my hands up to the sky and shrug. "Tricks or treats."

"You didn't *offer* us any treats." Hope's laughter betrays the scolding tone I think she wanted.

Lilly's clutching her chest and laughing. "You almost gave me a heart attack."

Guilt stabs between my ribs. Truly scaring them wasn't the goal.

"I was waiting for Rooster, but you two delicious little morsels were too tempting to pass up." I glance around at the crowded parking lot. "Plus, you came the closest to me. And why should the kids have all the fun?"

"How long were you planning to hang up there?" Hope asks.

"As long as it took." The rig actually has a small platform, so it's not like I was really *hanging*. I've endured worse for far less noble reasons.

"Jiggy, what the hell?" Z shouts, jogging over the blacktop.

Oh shit.

Punishment due.

"Gotta run, ladies!" I rip off my costume pants, brush off the hay and sprint toward the next parking lot. My bike's parked in front of Wrath's gym. Maybe I can circle around the building and make my escape.

Z's boots thunder behind me.

"Z, don't!" Lilly shouts.

I risk glancing over my shoulder. Z's fast but my president has like ten years on me. I'm younger and faster. I can outrun him.

At least I think I can.

CHAPTER EIGHT

Lilly

I can't remember the last time I laughed so hard.

"Oh my God, I needed this so bad today," I say, wiping tears from my eyes.

Hope and I are still clinging to each other, laughing hysterically.

Z races up to us. "You okay?"

"We're fine—"

Fury twists his face. He doesn't realize Jiggy was playing a harmless prank.

"Z, don't!" I shout as he tears after Jigsaw.

"Jeez," Hope groans. "Poor Jiggy went to a lot of effort just to get his ass kicked."

"Z better not," I mutter, watching the two of them zigzagging through the parking lot next door.

"Let's go see if we can intercept them in the front of the building." Hope tugs on my hand, pulling me forward.

We run into Rock first. Chance races over and hugs my legs.

"What the fuck was that all about?" Rock asks.

Hope takes Grace from him, kissing her daughter's cheeks. "Jigsaw pranked us."

"We heard you two screaming from across the parking lot."

Hope blushes. "He got us good, I'll admit."

I can't stop laughing. "Come on, let's go save Jiggy."

Z and Jigsaw land in the narrow strip of grass between the two businesses, rolling around like kids on a playground.

Hope and I skirt around the unmanned pumpkin carving station and approach Z and Jigsaw.

"Ow! Prez, it was an innocent prank. They're laughing, look!" Jiggy points wildly in our direction.

"Z." I walk up and touch his shoulder. "We're fine. We had a good laugh."

Z grins at me and jumps up off of Jigsaw. "Your ol' man still has it."

"Has what?" Hope asks.

"Strength, speed, and skill."

From the ground, Jiggy rolls over and cough-laughs. "I *let* you catch me, old man."

I blow out a breath and shake my head. "Everything's been all about the kids. Jigsaw was just trying to do something funny to include us in the festivities." Boy, I'm really pulling stuff out of my ass here.

"See?" Jigsaw winks at me and shoots a smug grin at Z.

Z grabs me by the hips and yanks me forward. "Trust me. He's not that deep."

I rest my hands on his shoulders and lean in closer. "I think you underestimate him sometimes," I say in a low voice.

He pulls me closer and bends down to whisper in my ear, "I fucking love you, Siren."

Suddenly, the October breeze seems impossibly hot.

"Can't you two go fornicate elsewhere? This is a children's event," Jiggy says.

Hope smacks his shoulder.

"What the fuck's going on out here?" Wrath bellows from behind us.

Z backs away but keeps his arms around my waist. "Just teaching my road captain a lesson in respect."

I roll my eyes.

"Well, teach him a lesson in manning his pumpkin carving station." Wrath jabs an angry finger toward the empty booth. "I want all those pumpkins out of my parking lot by tonight."

"I wanna pumpkin!" Chance jumps up and down.

His excitement renews Grace's interest in the activities, and she squirms for Hope to set her down.

I capture Chance's hand before he can run off. "Hold Grace's hand," I tell him.

Jiggy steps by us, giving Z a wide berth. Chance tugs and squirms to get loose from me.

"Follow Uncle Jigsaw," I say.

Hanging onto Grace, Chance throws me a look I

interpret as "duh, where else would we go" and follows Jiggy. Just in case, Wrath trails behind them.

They stop to inspect the pumpkins.

"You're really okay?" Z asks, reclaiming my attention.

"Yes, you overprotective caveman."

"You say that like it's an insult."

Hope titters with laughter. "I think I peed my pantaloons when he recited that creepy poem."

I burst out laughing. "Pantaloons? Jesus, Hope."

"Poem?" Rock lifts an eyebrow.

"Jigsaw's full of surprises," Z groans. "I swear, every day I unlock some new, ghoulish factoid about him."

"I think," I poke Z in the chest, "he's blossoming under your leadership. Sway didn't appreciate his uniqueness. Now, Jigsaw feels freer to be himself."

Hope lets out a low whistle. "You really need to return to politics, Lilly."

"That's some amazing bullshit," Z agrees.

I grin at both of them. "Spin wasn't my specialty."

"You're damn good at it, though," Rock says, taking Hope's hand. The two of them head for the pumpkins, leaving us alone.

"Hey," Z says, resting his forehead against mine. "Thank you."

"For?"

"Being the best damn ol' lady a president could ask for."

"How's that?"

He shrugs and stares up at the brilliant blue October sky for a moment as if he's trying to find the right words.

"Sticking up for a brother. Accepting their quirks with class and grace." He steps back and sweeps his gaze over my black turtleneck and jeans. "And looking really fucking hot while doing it."

"Love the man, love the club," I murmur.

"Yeah. I know that's not always easy."

"Sometimes it's fun, though." I tilt my head toward the pumpkins. Alexa's joined Chance and Grace. The three of them are sitting together on a big bale of hay, listening intently to Jigsaw.

"Three pumpkins were sitting on a gate.

The biggest one says, "It's getting late!"

The medium one says, "But there are witches and ghosts floating in the air."

The smallest one says, "I'm not scared!"

Tiny little giggles float through the air.

"I'm da biggest and I not scared!" Chance announces.

"Where does Jigsaw come up with this shit?" Z groans.

"It's cute. Look how enthralled the kids are."

He sighs and kisses my forehead. "Man, the rage that went through me when I heard you scream...it's a good thing you tried to stop me. By the time I caught up to him, I wasn't as pissed."

"Hope and I were finishing our conversation about my run-in with Sophie, so honestly, it was a perfect distraction."

"How'd that go?" he asks.

"Like you said, she wasn't bothered at all."

"Good." He grits his teeth. "Let's go to dinner at your

family's Sunday. For your brother. Anyone starts ragging on you, we'll just get up and leave."

I consider the offer, appreciating it more than I can express, but in my heart, it's not what I want. At all. "Nah." I scan the parking lot. My gaze lands on Trinity and I lift my hand to wave at her. "Trinity has a whole autumn-themed menu planned for Sunday." I meet Z's eyes again. "I don't want to miss family dinner night with my *true* family. But thank you for offering."

"Lilly?" His voice drops to a serious tone. "You realize I'd burn the world to the ground for you."

"I know." I lean up and kiss his cheek. "And that's why I'd do the same for you."

CHAPTER NINE

Ravage

Halloween Party
New Empire Clubhouse

EXHAUSTION PULLS ME UPSTAIRS. WE'VE GOT A FEW hours before the party officially kicks off, but I've been awake for the last twenty-four hours pulling things together. The clubhouse is currently full of kids and ol' ladies, which is cool and all, they were invited. But it seems like a safe time to escape for a nap.

I jog up the stairs, heading for the room at the end of the hallway. Even though we reserved a room for each officer, fuck knows none of them have ever spent a night here. Rock said he didn't care if I used his room. He hasn't even stepped foot in the suite since the first open house we had to celebrate the new space.

At the door, I stop and listen.

Is that water running? Or noise from downstairs?

Probably noise from one of the other rooms.

I twist the key in the lock and push the door open. This suite isn't as grand as the room Rock and Hope share at the compound. Construction costs were through the roof, so we chose function over fancy shit like we have at the main clubhouse. But at least we can behave like a real MC here, instead of a Brady Bunch family reunion every damn night.

Although, I have to admit, I'm fond of family dinner nights. And Z's son is kinda cool when he lets you play with his toy cars. The kid has like a million of 'em.

But *here* we can have as many girls as we want hang out and not have to worry about them dissing the ol' ladies or starting shit. Because when it comes to disrespecting one of my brother's ol' ladies, I'm always going to side with the ol' lady, and that makes it difficult to get my dick sucked in peace.

Anyway, inside the room there's a king-sized bed—of course—a dresser, and a flat-screen television. What more does a man need? To my right there's a small closet and the door to the attached bathroom.

Huh. Why's the bathroom door closed?

My gaze drops to the floor and light is spilling underneath. A shadow crosses the light.

The bathroom doorknob twists and creaks.

Fuck, someone's in there.

I beat a hasty retreat but I'm not quick enough.

Hope emerges with a short, white towel wrapped around her curvy body. Her long hair's twisted into a knot on top of her head but little sprigs escaped, water dripping from the ends.

Must. Not. Look. At. President's. Wife.

Naked.

Skin.

Pale, creamy skin flushed pink from her shower. Oh fuck.

Whoever bought the towels for the clubhouse deserves a medal. The thing's too small to fully wrap all the way around Hope's impressive chest, so a wide slit gives me a view of bare thigh and hip. None of the good stuff, yet. Although, if she moves another inch to the left, I might—

Rock's going to murder me.

It'll be worth it, though.

"Ravage!" Hope gasps. "Oh my gosh." She jumps backward—an impressive leap that unfortunately for me doesn't dislodge the already loose towel.

"Sorry, sorry, sorry." *Shit, fuck. What did I just do?* "I'm sorry, Hope."

I hurry into the hallway, slamming the door behind me.

Can't. Unsee.

I press my back against the wall and close my eyes. All I see is drops of water running over bare thigh.

"She's a dolphin, she's a dolphin, she's a dolphin," I mutter to myself over and over.

It's not working. Z's theory that a brother's ol' lady can't possibly be hot because once she's claimed, she's a dolphin is a total fucking scam. I can't picture Hope as anything other than hot, wet, and almost naked.

Rock's gonna kill me slowly.

"She's a dolphin, she's a—"

"What the fuck are you doing, Rav?" Rock's deadly calm voice cuts through my useless chanting.

Thank God I haven't eaten yet, or I'd shit my pants.

"Nothing." I open my eyes and distance myself from the door.

Rock frowns as his piercing gaze settles over me. "You okay?"

"Yup," I answer, a few octaves higher than normal. "Peachy. Groovy. All good in the hood."

Rock's frown deepens. He adjusts the backpack slung over his shoulder. Christ, what are the chances he's got a weapon in there? Will he beat me to death or just shoot me and be done with it? We've buried more than a few bodies together. Rock's capable of digging a deep grave without breaking a sweat.

"Things look good outside and downstairs," he says.

"Thanks."

I gotta get out of here. No, if I run, it'll look too obvious. Guilty or something.

Maybe change the subject? Or should I just confess and get it over with? If I tell him before Hope does, maybe he won't kill me.

What do I say? "Your wife is smoking hot?" Nope, that'll definitely get me killed.

Is there any chance Hope won't tell him that I walked in on her? Nah, I did more than walk in on her. I stood there and stared like a fucking creep. Took in every inch my stupid, greedy eyes dared. I'm so dead.

"Where's the baby?" I curl my arms together and swing them from side to side in front of me in case Rock has no idea what I mean by *baby*. Jesus, this just keeps getting worse.

He jerks his thumb over his shoulder. "Downstairs with Heidi and Murphy. Hope came up here to change into her other costume."

"Oh," I squeak like a preteen whose balls haven't dropped yet. "Cool. Cool."

Keeping my back to the wall, I slide a few feet away from Rock. "I, uh, gotta get downstairs now." Maybe flee the country.

Rock's piercing gray eyes stab me all the way to the staircase.

I grip the banister. Safety's a few skips away.

The scrape of a key in the lock reaches me. I hesitate and turn my head. Rock has his hand curled around the knob.

"Hey, Prez?" I call out.

He turns and our eyes meet.

"I'm really glad you guys came to the party." I flash him a thumbs-up. "and you're a very lucky man."

His eyes widen. He pauses, then takes a step toward me.

I run down the stairs like death's hot on my ass.

CHAPTER TEN

Rock

THE URGE TO CHASE RAVAGE DOWN AND CHOKE SOME answers out of him takes a back seat to my concern for Hope.

I turn the knob and step into "our room" at the new clubhouse. Sparsely furnished—I'd told Rav I really didn't give a fuck what was in here—but clean, it vaguely smells like pine air freshener.

Light spills under the bathroom door to my right. I tap my knuckles against the hollow wood.

"Rock?" Hope's timid question sparks my anger. I'm going to kill Rav. I don't know why yet, but he's definitely dead.

"It's me."

The door opens. A curtain of wet hair clings to her shoulders and falls down her back. In her hand, she's toying with a large hair clip. A towel's tightly wrapped over her breasts. My gaze travels over her. She's so damn beautiful, for a second I forget about the weird encounter with Ravage. My fingers tingle with the urge to rip the towel out of my way.

Then I take in the bright red of her squeaky-clean skin. The flush runs from her chest to her forehead. More than the pink she gets from a hot shower.

"What happened?" I ask.

"Ugh." She rolls her eyes. "I don't want to tell you."

She seems more embarrassed than upset. "Why?"

"I don't want you to kill Ravage."

"I'll decide if he needs to die or not." I lift my hand, wiggling my fingers in a "give me the facts" gesture.

She grabs her comb off the sink and pushes past me into the bedroom, softly padding to the door and checking that it's locked. Satisfied no one will bust in, she perches on the edge of the bed and runs the comb through her hair. The towel gaps at the side, giving me a clear view up to her hip.

"Nothing. It's stupid," she says. "Rav must've thought the room was empty. He walked in when I got out of the shower—"

"He *what?*"

"Not like that." She waves her comb toward the bathroom. "I had my towel on but jeez, they really skimped on the towels for the clubhouse. This thing barely covers my boobs."

"Still too much fabric for my taste," I growl. "Or not. Continue."

"That's it. I think he was as shocked as I was. We stood there staring at each other." She flicks the comb through her hair even faster. "He'll probably go tell the other guys all about my gross mom body."

I pinch the bridge of my nose. "There's nothing gross about you."

"*I* didn't say there was." Her lips curl into a seductive smile. "I look fucking amazing."

"Yes, you do." I run my gaze over her again.

"But," she adds with an annoyed huff, "he's used to twenty-year-old stripper bodies and that's not me."

"And thank fuck for that." I give her a hard stare. "You realize his opinion's irrelevant, right? If I ever caught him saying something bad about you, he'd be dead in a heartbeat."

"Oh, I know."

I can't help the smirk forming on my face. "Besides, when he got far enough away from me, he shouted that I was a lucky man."

Soft laughter spills past her lips. "Probably to save you from killing him when you found out."

"Nah." Enough of this. Words don't work with my woman. I need to *show* her exactly how lucky I feel that she's mine. "Take that towel off," I demand.

"This?" She teases her fingers along the edge of the thin, white terry cloth.

"Yes," I growl, stripping off my cut and draping it over the end of the bed.

She inches away from me, scooting toward the pillows.

"Where do you think you're going?" I wrap my hand around one of her ankles and yank her to the edge, dislodging the towel in the process.

She tugs the towel out from underneath her and tosses it aside. "Trinity's going to be up here soon. We're supposed to get ready together."

"She'll wait." My hungry eyes devour every naked inch of my wife.

"Well, in that case, this doesn't seem fair." She snags her fingers in my belt and yanks me forward.

"You want it off, take it off."

Her mouth curls into a playful smile. I reach down and cup her cheek, tipping her head back. I run my thumb over her bottom lip. "First, tell me something you love about yourself, baby doll."

She blinks and stares up at me. Odd request, maybe. But no matter how she tried to explain it away, that *gross mom body* comment is still bugging me.

She takes her hands off my belt and leans back on her elbows, giving me an incredible view. I'm dying to drop to my knees and worship her the way she deserves.

But first, I want an answer.

She trails her fingers between her breasts and over her stomach. "The way you feel inside me."

Fuck me. She's going to test every ounce of restraint I have. "Nice try," I answer as coolly as possible. "But that's about me. Not you."

She lifts one shoulder. "It's about *us*."

I never tire of her challenging me and I'm an extremely patient man. I cock an eyebrow, quietly letting her know she's not getting out of answering my question.

She lets out a long, slow breath and turns her head. "I love my hair. Trinity suggested a blonde wig to complete my costume but I said no. *This* Sandy is going to have auburn curls."

I reach down and run my hand over the damp strands, slowly drying into loose waves. "I'm glad. I love your hair too."

"Satisfied?" she asks. Stretching out on the bed, she arches her back, thrusting her tits up in a way she knows I can't resist. One of her hands slides between her legs. "Are you going to give me a treat or do I need to treat myself?"

I fall down over her, covering her body with my own. "You play dirty."

She loops her arms around my neck and playfully pouts. "I know."

I dip my head, pressing my lips to hers. She opens for me immediately, stroking her tongue against mine. Her arms lock around my neck, holding me in place like she's determined to kiss every thought in my head away.

I shift us onto the mattress better, then dip my head to take one perky, pink nipple in my mouth, sliding my tongue over the tip.

Underneath me she gasps and lifts her legs, hugging her knees to my hips. I pull back. "What's wrong?"

Instead of answering, she slides her hands between our bodies, going for my belt again. One of her hands slides lower, cupping my painfully hard cock.

"You hit just the right spot and I need you inside me. *Now.*"

I'm fighting a battle I'll never win. "I'm not ready, baby doll."

"The hell you're not," she mutters, finally working my belt loose.

Rumbling with laughter, I take my weight off her and strip off my shirt. "That's not what I meant."

"Mmm, much better." She slides her hands over my stomach, my sides, and down my back. Her fingers like trails of fire flowing over my skin.

I trail kisses over her neck and chest. She shudders under me when I suck her nipple into my mouth again.

"Please," she whispers.

"Baby doll, I want to kiss every single inch of your body."

Her lips purse into the frustrated pout I can't resist. Finally, I take mercy on her and together we slide my jeans down.

"God, yes," she murmurs, curling her hands around my throbbing cock.

"Fuck." I squeeze my eyes shut, enjoying the sensation. She's right. Dragging this out isn't the way to go. I need to be inside her. Now. And judging by the way she's wrapping her legs around my waist, we're on the same page.

I shift my body and use one hand to guide the head of my cock right where I need it. "Mine," I whisper against her neck.

"All yours. Now take me."

Laughing against her shoulder, I thrust deep inside her.

"Yes." Her eyes roll back.

I swear to fuck I need to count back from one hundred to keep from coming. Tight, wet, hot. *All mine, mine, mine.*

"You really were ready." I suck at a spot below her ear and she rolls her hips, encouraging me to move faster. I take a breath but fuck, she's got my dick in a stranglehold. "You sure we can't stay here all night?"

Hope

It's such a tempting offer. Grace is safe with her aunt and uncle. Rock and I have a brand-new bedroom to explore.

"We have all night." I press a quick kiss to his lips. "This is just to take the edge off. I promise to ride you hard later, Mr. President."

"You better." He slams his mouth against mine. A kiss full of need that steals my breath. Hard and demanding, just like everything about my husband. "I need you."

I live to be needed and loved by this man. I drag my nails over his back, exploring his hardness, admiring his restraint. "What's something you love about yourself?" I ask, echoing his earlier question.

"What?" He stares into my eyes. We're almost nose to nose. So close our breath mingles together. He shifts his hips. "You're strangling my dick and you want a coherent thought out of me?"

"Payback's a mean bitch, huh?" I tease. I glide my hands lower, lightly scratching his firm ass.

He tilts his head slightly, studying his heavily inked bicep. "My strength," he answers. "Knowing I can protect you and Grace." A bloodthirsty light enters his stormy eyes. "Beat the shit out of anyone who threatens your peace."

Such savage, yet romantic, words.

And I knew he wasn't over the whole Ravage walking in here thing.

"Yes," I agree. "I love how hard you can fuck me too."

A primitive growl claws its way out of his throat. "Enough talking. All I want to hear is the sound of your wet cunt draining my cock."

I'm no longer capable of forming words anyway. He moves slower this time, sweet punishment for interrupting him with my question. He glides in and out of me with precision. So determined to bring both of us pleasure. I hitch my hips higher and curl my hands around his forearms.

"God, right there," I whisper.

"That's my girl," he groans.

My thoughts scatter. Complete magic. Tingles whisper over my skin. Every nerve ending in my body sparks. Bliss rolls in, filling my mind like a fog I never want to work my way out of. My orgasm explodes through me, sending trembles down my legs. I turn my head, sinking my teeth into his arm.

"Ah, fuck!" he groans, burying himself inside me.

Above me, his body stills as his face contorts in pleasure. A triumphant shout, followed by a groan. My legs continue shaking as we ride out our releases together.

CHAPTER ELEVEN

Trinity

A SENSE OF ACCOMPLISHMENT FILLS MY CHEST AS WE close and lock the doors of Furious Fitness. "That went well," I say to Wrath, holding up the sticky note where I quickly wrote down the amount we'd raised for charity from today's event. "We collected a lot of canned goods and beauty supplies too. Heidi's going to help me drop them off on Friday."

He slings his arm over my shoulders and hugs me to him. "Thanks to you," he says, leaning down to kiss my cheek.

"Not just me." I reach for Carter, who's a few steps ahead of us. "Thank you. The scenes you painted were so pretty, I didn't want to take them down."

Carter blushes and ducks his head. "Thanks."

"You did good, Scribbles." Wrath thumps Carter on the back a few times.

"Easy," Carter wheezes, holding out the foot that was

injured not that long ago. "I don't quite have my balance back."

"You want a piggyback ride?" Wrath offers, only half-serious, I think.

"I want to forget that whole night happened," Carter groans.

"You're coming with us to the clubhouse, right?" I ask.

He shrugs. "I don't really have a costume."

Wrath tugs at the sleeves of his flannel. "I'm going like this." He glances down at me. "Except for Jiggy, I think only the girls are going in costume."

"Teller wanted me to help at the house," Carter offers.

Wrath yanks his phone out. "You've done enough work today." He taps out a text. "Scribbles is riding with us to the party," he reads as his thumbs move across the screen. "There. He won't argue with me."

"I have my car," Carter says, waving his arm toward the parking lot.

"So, you'll follow us," Wrath says. "Come on. Rav wants you there."

"He does?" Carter asks.

"Yeah."

"Let's go," I urge. "I'm supposed to help Hope with her hair, Lilly with her makeup, and I need them to help me with something." I grab Wrath's hand and tug him toward the parking lot.

The ride to the new clubhouse isn't far. I check my mirror to make sure Carter's still following.

I tuck my Jeep into a spot by the side door. The new

building feels somewhere between a dorm and a house. Not that I ever went to college and lived in a dorm. Just based off of television and movies.

Outside, Wrath joins me and takes my hand. It's not quite dark yet but the twelve-foot Frankenstein and fake tombstones in front of the building are already lit up.

"They must've been busy decorating," I say to Wrath.

"Rav really wants to prove himself to Rock," he answers in a low voice. "To all of us, I guess."

"Well, he did a stellar job." I flick a tiny spider nestled in a cotton spiderweb as we enter the front door.

"Swan said it was a horror movie theme," Carter says.

My gaze quickly scans the room. What I hope is a fake skull sits on a bed of orange maple leaves over the fireplace. Spooky fog rolls over the floor. Flashing lights, skeletons, monsters, coffins, bats, and all sorts of decorations surround us. "You mean every horror movie ever?" I ask.

Carter nods.

Swan—decked out in a sparkling black feather tutu—runs up and hugs me. "I'm so glad you're here. How'd it go?"

"Great! We raised a lot of money." I search the room again. Where the hell is Hope?

Swan and Carter disappear into the fog. Wrath tugs me to the side, out of the way of the front door. "I see Grinder and Serena," he shouts over the opening notes of the theme song to *The Exorcist*.

"Oh good. Lead us that way."

Grinder and Rooster are deep in conversation while Serena's sitting on the couch, touching up Shelby's makeup.

"What the heck is Serena's costume?" Wrath mutters to me.

"I don't know. Be nice," I warn him.

He peers down at me. "I'm always nice."

Serena struggles to get off the couch when we approach. But Grinder's right there to offer his assistance, gently easing her to her feet.

"Girl, are you ready to pop yet?" I ask.

"Almost." She grins.

I take in her costume of what looks like white gauze wrapped around her from neck to toes, a stylish white turban and black-and-white makeup. The woman's a million months pregnant and looks stunning. "What are you?"

She rubs her hand over her belly in an affectionate circle. "Mummy to be!"

"Oh my God." I snort-laugh. "Damn, that's good."

Shelby pops up next to her. "You have to see Charlotte. She's so dang cute."

I check out Shelby's sparkly velvet and chiffon dress embroidered with silver stars and threads. A necklace of rainbow crystals at her neck and her face glammed out with silver makeup and rhinestones. "Fortune teller." Shelby shrugs. "My version."

"Pretty." I study her makeup again. "How long did that take?"

"Hours." She gestures at Serena. "We filmed the whole thing. It came out great."

Damn. I can apply some eyeliner and shadow well

enough to avoid looking like a clown, but Serena's skills are movie level.

Lilly touches my shoulder and gives me a quick hug. I'd barely had a chance to talk to her earlier. "Where's your costume?" I ask.

She points to the ceiling. "Z brought all our stuff up earlier." She pats Serena's back. "Her train case is literally the size of a train."

Serena giggles. "No it's not. I did bring a lot of stuff, though."

"Has anyone seen Hope?" I ask.

"Um, last we knew she went to take a shower," Lilly laughs. "We haven't seen her *or* Rock since."

"Oh, Christ," I mutter at the ceiling.

Serena points at Lilly. "Your face is going to take forever. Let's get going."

"You know what, I better check to see if Hope's decent," I say to the girls, pulling out my phone to send her a text. I notice she sent me a text earlier that I never saw or responded to. *Ooops.* "Did anyone bring curling irons?" I ask as I type out an *are you decent* text.

"I did!" Shelby volunteers. "I got this cool new auto-spinning one." She twirls her finger in the air. "At the press of a button."

"I brought a few," Serena says. "All different sizes."

"Oh good. I need a small-diameter one for Hope's hair. She said *absolutely not* to wearing a wig with her costume."

Shelby wrinkles her nose. "Don't blame her. It's already hot as Hades in here."

"I got you," Serena assures me.

I walk over to Wrath and tap his arm. "We're headed upstairs."

"Let me go with you," Grinder says to Serena. He tosses a worried glance at the staircase.

"You all right, Serena?" I ask.

"Yes, just a little big and clumsy."

"Shoot. I don't know if there's a room down here we can—"

"I'm fine," she says. "Gray's just being overprotective."

Lilly snorts. "It seems to be going around." She flashes a knowing smile at Grinder.

After another round of chatter, I finally herd the girls toward the stairs. On the way, we pass Birch in a pink bunny suit. Guessing he lost a bet. Someone, rather convincingly, had sunk a throwing star into the middle of Hoot's forehead. Fake blood from the "wound" trails down his nose and onto his white T-shirt.

Grinder and Serena follow us up the stairs at a slower pace. Ignoring the rest of the rooms, I march down the hallway and knock hard against the presidential suite's door. Lilly directs Serena and Shelby to the room she and Z are staying in, right next door.

Rock answers my knock—fully dressed, thank God. You never know with these two. "Hey, Trinny." He opens the door wider.

"What's shaking, Rock-around-the-clock?"

He chuckles at my greeting.

"Tell me she's ready?" I ask.

The bathroom door flies open and Hope steps out in the "Sandy" costume we'd ordered weeks ago. Skintight, shiny black pants cinched at the waist with a thin black belt fit perfectly. A tight black off-the-shoulder top flatters her curves. The red heels she bought to complete the outfit dangle from her fingers.

"The pants fit!" She spins for us. "All your nagging and dragging me to the gym at the butt-crack of dawn worked, Trinity. They fit!"

Rock runs his hand over his chin, staring at her for an uncomfortably long time. "Yes, they do."

"Oh boy," I mutter.

Hope stares at her nails. "I think I broke a nail squeezing my ass into them, though."

"It'll grow back." I grab her free hand and drag her toward the door. "Sorry, Rock. You can have your way with her later."

He follows behind us and meets up with Grinder in the hallway.

"Go check out the party, Rock," I suggest. "They did a great job."

"Yeah, I'm headed downstairs to do some hunting," he says rather cryptically.

He leaves with Grinder, and I shove Hope into our "get-ready" room.

"Easy. Why so pushy tonight?" she says over her shoulder.

"I saw your man eyeing you. And we all know what that leads to. You're not getting out of this party."

She blushes and doesn't deny it.

Inside the room, a long L-shaped table with lights and a mirror has been set up for us.

"My request," Serena says, nodding at the table. She starts digging through her makeup cases, neatly setting everything she wants on the table.

"All right. Let's curl your hair," I say to Hope.

"Oh dear." She eyes the chair at one end of the table. "I don't know if I can *sit* in these pants."

"Let's give it a try."

Shelby helps me curl Hope's hair which is a huge help. I tease and spray it into a fluffy ball and stick a red ribbon in the side.

Serena has some sort of fishnet template glued to Lilly's face and seems to be mapping out a design. "I didn't ask what your costume is, Lilly?" I ask.

"You'll see."

"Don't move," Serena warns.

While they're busy doing that, I grab my outfit—a sleeveless, shiny red catsuit. "Now it's time to help me into this thing," I say to Hope. She'd helped me plan the outfit a few weeks ago and knew this was coming.

"What is it?" Shelby asks.

"Bad angel?" I shrug. "I was a good angel all day. Now I get to be naughty."

Hope chuckles. "Wrath's going to lose his mind."

"I know." I grin and glance at my bag. "My last costume of the night is a much tinier version for his eyes only."

"I don't need to know that," she moans.

We step into the bathroom and Hope closes the door. "All right. What do I need to do?" She claps her hands together and stares at the costume, all business now.

"Don't laugh, but it came with a special kind of lube to help it slide on easier."

She ignores my "don't laugh" warning and falls into a fit of giggles.

"Just help me tug it into place," I huff. "I think it'll be easier because it's sleeveless."

"And strapless. Aren't you worried your boobs will fall out?"

"Nah, we'll wrestle them into place."

"I love you, Trin," she says in a voice full of false patience. "You've already got me lubing you up. But I draw the line at boob-wrangling."

"Sheesh." I'd prepped the suit earlier, but it needs smoothing out.

I strip down to my underwear and start the process. Thanks to the lube, the suit goes on easier than I expected. "Cinch it tight, Hope," I say over my shoulder as she works the ties up the back.

"I don't want to crush your ribs." She grunts and pulls harder.

"You won't," I assure her.

Finally, we're done. I turn and hold out my arms. "What do you think?"

"Hot, hot, hot." She shakes her head. "Fire in human form."

"Thanks." I smooth my hands over my hips.

We join the others and Hope helps me strap a pair of red, feathers-and-sequins wings on my back.

"Damn, Trinity," Lilly says, running her hand over the leg of my suit. "This is amazing."

"Thanks." I search the room. "I need my halo."

"Oh, hang on." Hope runs out of the room and returns a few seconds later with her hands behind her back.

"What's that?" I ask.

She holds out a gold crown with sparkling red stones. "Instead of a halo, I thought you deserved a crown. You are a LOKI queen, after all."

"Queen of the bad angels. I love it," Shelby hoots.

Well, at least if I start crying, I won't ruin my makeup since I haven't put any on yet.

"Damn it, Hope." I take the crown and study the shiny gold metal and ruby-red crystals. "It's really pretty. Thank you."

"We're almost done," Serena says. "So whoever needs me next, come on over."

Lilly's been transformed. Serena painted a full mask of glittery blue and green fish-like scales from Lilly's forehead to the apples of her cheeks. Below that, she's painted an outline of a skull, complete with a freakish number of white teeth stretched almost from ear to ear.

"Mermaid skeleton?" I guess.

"Yup. My dress is in the closet."

"If you need to be lubed up, I'm now an expert," Hope offers.

"Hope, we all know you don't need lube with Rock," Lilly says sweetly. "The man looks at you and—"

"Shut up." Hope laughs. "I meant if you need help getting into the dress. Never mind."

Serena's still laughing when I take the chair in front of her. "How do you feel about falsies?" she asks me.

I stare at her with a blank expression, then glance at my boobs. "I don't think I need anything additional in that department."

"No! False *lashes*. I have this red feather pair that would be so perfect with that outfit. I've been saving them for something special."

"No, I don't want to—"

"Please," she pleads. "They'll look so good on you."

"Just say yes, Trin," Shelby warns in a low, confidential tone.

Serena grins and nods vigorously.

"Okay," I agree.

"They might be a little heavy." Serena leans to the side to search her train case for the lashes.

Finally, she presents a gold, glittery rectangular box to me. Two crescents of tiny red feathers with curled edges rest inside. I don't know a lot about makeup stuff, but they look expensive.

"Are you sure? You don't want to save them for yourself?"

"No! I have so many, I'll never use them all."

"All right." *Why not?*

"Yay!" She lets out a happy squeal. Then, a pang of guilt

105

creeps over me. I've known Serena for years, but we've only gotten close since she hooked up with Grinder.

I reach over and rest my hand over hers. "I'm glad you came tonight."

"Grayson said it was mandatory," she says with an affectionate smile.

I'm not getting my point across. The touchy-feely stuff will never be my specialty.

"Look down," Serena orders.

First, she pats shadow over my lids, then lines my eyes.

"Time for lashes!" she chirps.

Her touch is gentle even if the process is a bit uncomfortable.

"Don't blink," she warns.

"All right," Lilly announces. "What do you think?"

"Serena says I can't open my eyes," I mutter.

"Talk about dangerous curves." Hope whistles. "Wow, Lilly."

"Okay, you can look," Serena says.

I peel my eyes open. The left one feels like it's lifting weights and every time I blink, I get a flash of red.

"Feel okay?" Serena asks.

"Just a little weird." I flick my gaze to Lilly and let out my own whistle. A sleek, deep blue, sequined strapless dress falls to her ankles, the skirt flaring out at the bottom. White "bones" have been embroidered into the front of the dress. Instead of legs, there's the outline of a tail. "Damn, woman. How can you make a skeleton look sexy?"

Lilly places her hands on her hips and strikes a dramatic pose. "It's a gift."

The girls snort-giggle and heckle Lilly.

"Let's finish," Serena says, touching my chin and turning me to face her. "Eyes closed," she reminds me.

Someone's phone buzzes.

"Rooster's got my fortune teller booth all set up," Shelby says. "I'm gonna head down there."

"Okay," Serena says to me. "You can open your eyes."

I blink them open for the second time.

"Feel okay?" Serena asks.

"I think so."

"You'll get used to them," Shelby assures me. "I wear them onstage all the time." She comes closer. "Ooo, never any as pretty as those, though. You girls all right if I head downstairs?"

"I'll go with you," Lilly volunteers. "Scope out the party."

"Let me finish your liner," Serena says. "Then it's your turn, Hope."

Hope stares down at her outfit. "Next to the four of you, I feel so uncreative in my totally plain costume."

"Yeah, but you look hot as fuck," Lilly says. "And anyone over twenty-five should know who you're supposed to be without asking."

"Hey!" Shelby raises her hand. "I'm under twenty-five and I know who Sandy Olsson is. I must've watched that movie a hundred times when I was a kid."

"Sorry," Lilly says. "Bottom line, we're all fucking hot."

CHAPTER TWELVE

Rock

I HAVEN'T GONE HUNTING WITH WRATH IN YEARS. BUT I still know a thing or two about stalking prey.

"What crawled up your ass, Rock?" Grinder asks.

"Nothing. Just need to find someone."

"G!" Rooster calls out. "Can you give me a hand?"

With Grinder occupied, I'm free to search the room.

There he is.

Ravage is leaning up against the wall, chatting up some girl in what I guess is a bunny costume. Tall white ears on her head, white bikini top, thong, and I don't want to contemplate how she attached the fluffy white tail coming out of her ass.

The muffler bunny turns and catches sight of me. Her eyes widen and she thrusts her chest out.

Rav frowns, confused about losing her attention. He follows her line of sight and it's almost comical how wide his eyes get.

He slips around the corner, hurrying away from me.

I move faster through the crowd, shouldering people out of my way.

"Oh, hi! You're Rock, right? The president?" the girl Rav had been talking to asks.

"Not now," I growl, moving past her. At least she chose her costume well.

Kitchen. I bet that's where the fucker's headed.

"What's wrong, Prez?" Hoot asks as I pass him. "Prez?" he calls again.

I stop and turn. "You seen Ravage?"

"Yeah." He points down the hallway. "Saw him go into the kitchen like three minutes ago."

I snarl and keep moving. This clubhouse has a more open design. No door closing off the dining room and kitchen like we have at the compound. I have a good view of the kitchen. It's large by most standards. Meant to prepare meals for twenty or more people.

More barely dressed girls I don't recognize mill around, preparing snacks and drinks. I catch sight of Rav ducking into the pantry.

Gotcha, fucker.

I don't have to dodge the girls, they trip over themselves to jump out of my way. So close now. I reach out and grab the collar of Rav's cut, yanking him backward.

His arms pinwheel out, scrambling for something to help keep him on his feet. Boxes of cereal spill to the floor. His boots slide in the mess, and he ends up on his ass. Keeping my hand fisted in his cut, I step around him. He stares up at me with wide-eyed panic.

"Prez." He holds his hands up in the air. "Let me explain."

I unsheathe my hunting knife, then squat so we're eye-level and tap the blade against his leg. "Give me a reason not to slice off your nuts and feed them to you as punishment for walking in on my ol' lady?"

He stares at the knife and slaps his hands over his crotch to shield himself. "It was an accident! I swear. I didn't even realize you guys were at the clubhouse yet. You know I'd never do anything to disrespect you or Hope," he says in a desperate rush of words.

I release him but keep the knife pointed at his junk.

"I'm really attached to my nuts, Prez," he pleads. "And, uh, I haven't decided if I wanna have kids one day."

Am I really going to mutilate him? Probably not. Do I want to scare him into learning how to knock before entering? Absolutely.

"What'd I miss, Rock?" Wrath rumbles from above us.

Ravage squeezes his eyes shut like the grim reaper just arrived to collect him.

I glance up at Wrath looming over us, arms crossed over his chest. His expression's blank. Hard and calculating. Punishments are usually his responsibility.

"Not your concern," I say.

He flicks his gaze at Rav, then at the knife in my hand. "Now I see why the girls freaked out and came looking for me." He taps Ravage's leg with his boot. "What'd you do now, fuckwit?"

I point the knife at Rav's face and cock my head, daring him to say a word.

He wisely keeps his mouth shut.

"Seems you have things handled." Wrath turns and walks away.

I tuck my knife into its sheath and stand. Rav eyes me carefully, then slowly picks himself up off the floor.

"If I hear that you ran your mouth about what you saw up there to anyone," I warn, "you won't see me coming."

"I swear. My lips are superglued."

"If you make things awkward for Hope or upset her in any way, I'll nail your nuts to the wall as a trophy. We clear?"

"Crystal clear." He stares at the sheath at my side. "Are we good now?"

I silently count to ten before answering, "We're good."

"It really was an accident—"

"No." I hold up one hand. "What we're *not* going to do is ever discuss this again. You feel me?"

"Yeah."

"And you're gonna learn to fucking knock on a closed fucking bedroom door from now on."

"Yes, Prez."

I tilt my head toward the kitchen. "Go."

He glances behind him. "Uh, you're not going to tell anyone, are you? Wrath and Murphy aren't going to take me out back and shoot me later, right?"

I'll probably tell Wrath. Otherwise, he'll annoy the fuck

out of me. And Hope might tell Trinity, which is as good as telling Wrath. As much as he enjoys being an asshole, if I tell Wrath it's handled and to leave it alone, he will. Rav doesn't need to know that, though.

My mouth curves into my coldest smile and I slowly lift my shoulders. "Live in fear, brother."

CHAPTER THIRTEEN
Charlotte

"WE'VE DONE OUR DUTY. IT'S TIME TO GO." MARCEL presses his hand against the small of my back. "I don't want you breathing in all this smoke and shit."

I lift my gaze to the high ceilings and fans circulating above. "The windows are open. Ventilation is good. I feel fine."

"I don't want to leave Murphy and Heidi watching all the kids by themselves."

"I'm pretty sure the kids are sound asleep." I pull my phone out of my purse and show him the picture Heidi sent me. The three older kids nestled into sleeping bags on our living room floor and baby Bit-Bit snuggly in her daddy's arms.

Marcel grunts at the picture but a flicker of a smile passes over his lips.

"Why are you so bugged about being here?"

He stares at me and frowns, like he's trying to figure out

the answer himself. "They built it to be their little den of deviance and that part of my life is behind me."

I snort and then full-out laugh. "You're kidding, right?" I lean up and whisper in his ear, "You're probably the biggest deviant in this room."

One corner of his mouth tips up and he nods to one of his brothers in the corner with a girl on her knees in front of him. "You sure?"

"That's just showing off." I scan the room. "Have you seen Carter?"

"Worried he's going to be corrupted?"

"That ship has sailed." I roll my eyes. "I don't live in older sibling fantasyland like you do."

He chuckles and puts his arm around me.

"Come on," I say, "I want to have Shelby read my fortune before we leave."

"I know your fortune. Your deviant husband's going to love you for a very long time. And if you die before me, I'm jumping in your grave."

"How perfectly romantic for Halloween."

Together, we walk over to Shelby's booth. People stop us to say hi. A guy I don't recognize tries to rub my belly. Marcel shackles his hand around the guy's wrist.

"You want this back?" he asks, shaking the guy's arm. "Don't touch my wife."

"Sorry, sorry." He backs away from us fast.

"Who the fuck *are* all these people?" Marcel grouches.

"Friends of Ravage's, I guess." I turn my head, searching the room. "Where is he, by the way?"

"No clue. But as soon as I talk to him, we're out of here."

I'm starting to agree with him but after making such a fuss about staying, I don't want to admit it.

"I see an ass-kickin' in your future if you don't back the fuck up." Shelby's Southern twang burns through all the other noise around us.

"Jesus," Marcel grumbles. "What now?"

Without even looking for Rooster, Marcel steps up to the man sitting at Shelby's table and taps him on the shoulder. "What's goin' on?"

The man isn't wearing a cut. He's dressed like Santa and glares at Teller for about two seconds. Recognition seems to cross his face and he jumps out of his seat.

"Nothing, man. Just talking to the lady. Thought that's what the girls were here for."

"She's my brother's ol' lady. You need to move along," Marcel says. "Now."

"Yeah, yeah. I'm goin', man."

Santa shuffles away, but Marcel isn't content with that. He searches the room. When his gaze lands on Wrath he signals to him.

"Give me a sec, Sunshine. I'll be right back." Marcel guides me into the chair across from Shelby and takes off.

"You all right?" I ask her.

"Pfft. I'm fine. He was just gross. Probably old enough to be my damn grandpa." She closes her eyes and takes several deep breaths, waving her hands back and forth. "Okay! Do you want me to pull cards for you?"

"Sure." I've watched Shelby do this several times and I'm still not sure what to think about the process.

"Good." She picks up her cards and starts shuffling them. "Do you have a question in mind?"

"Not really."

"That's okay." She sets the cards in front of me, splits the deck, and fans the cards out. "Pick three."

I touch several cards before pulling three out and handing them to her. She picks up the rest of the cards, setting them to the side.

One by one, she turns over the cards. A sly smile curves her pink lips.

"The universe is feeling obvious tonight. Empress." She taps the card with a woman wearing a crown. "A sign of fertility."

I rub my stomach. "I can think of another big sign."

"No joke." She taps the next card. "The Sun, for our family's sunshine—perfect. Can also indicate children or fertility. And finally, the Ace of Wands. It can mean new opportunities and growth."

"I'm definitely growing," I agree.

She picks the cards up. "That's a relief. I was worried that since I'm kinda doing this for kicks as a party trick, the readings would be garbage. But that was a dang good one."

I can't see how she could've rigged that to pull those particular cards for me. "I guess there's magic in the air tonight."

CHAPTER FOURTEEN

Wrath

A FEW DAYS AFTER HALLOWEEN...

After everyone's finished dinner, I stand and rap my knuckles against the table. Rock and I agreed to have an informal meeting that included everyone to discuss the Halloween party and charity event. Not exactly church, since everyone associated with the club was invited to family dinner night and therefore the meeting.

I glance at Rock who nods at me. For some reason, he gave me the honor of running the meeting. Something about how much I bitched when they chose Furious as the location of the charity event.

"This was the best meal." Rav kicks back, resting his boots on the table and holds up one hand to capture our attention. "Don't get offended, Swan."

Little fucker's been smug since Halloween.

Swan flashes a quick, patient smile at Ravage. "I'm listening."

Rav's eyes shift between Trinity and Swan. "This right here was even better than the food we had catered for the party."

Trinity beams.

"Why would that make us mad?" Swan asks.

He shrugs. "I know you worked hard on arranging it."

"Trinity and I worked harder on cooking this dinner," she points out. "So did Shelby and Lilly."

"I'm *still* finding butternut squash in my hair," Shelby mutters, twisting her head to check out her blonde curls.

"Worth every second," Jigsaw says.

"That's 'cause you didn't lose a fight with an immersion blender," Shelby says.

Rooster curls his arm around her shoulders and whispers something in her ear.

I lean over to Trinity. "You got any treats in your hair for me to find later?"

She snorts. "No."

"All right." I slap my palm against the table to get everyone's attention. "I'm only going to say this once."

Everyone at the table groans.

"I feel like we're about to be lectured," Sparky moans.

"Careful, Sparky." I flick my hand in his direction. "There's a faint beam of afternoon sunlight over there. Don't want you to burst into flames."

"So funny." He sticks his tongue out at me.

I tap Trinity's shoulder, to let her know it's her turn. "Checks were sent to both charities." She nods at Teller to confirm. "Murphy and Heidi dropped off the food and other donations to the shelter yesterday. They were really grateful to have so much donated."

"I gave all the receipts to Teller," Murphy adds. He glances at Teller then Downstate's treasurer, Hustler. "Not sure how you guys want to split that up."

"We'll work it out," Hustler says.

"We should collect donations again for Christmas," Bricks suggests.

"Sounds good," Rock says.

"Why just holidays?" Jigsaw asks. "Shelters, food pantries, they probably need stuff all year round."

"What do you wanna do, donate *all* your money?" Hustler asks. "What're you gonna fix up your hog with, then?"

Before they start bickering, I slap the table again.

Z lifts his hand. "Downstate can host the next event, so the whole burden doesn't fall on you guys."

"But we have the nicer clubhouse," Rav protests.

"Yeah, I'm cool with Ravage doing it," Butcher offers.

Rock sighs.

"Jigsaw," I say, wanting to return to his suggestion. "What do you have in mind?"

"Uh, I don't know." He taps his fingers against the table like he's wishing he never opened his mouth. "It just seems people only think about donating stuff around holidays and people need stuff all year round."

"We'll think on it," Rooster promises, leaning over to tap Jiggy's shoulder with his fist.

"We need to do a better job with the guest list," Teller

says. "Couple people there showed some disrespect to our ol' ladies and it wasn't cool."

Shelby lifts her hand. "I can confirm that one."

I flick my gaze to Ravage and smirk. His eyes widen. Rock gave me the short version of what went down. It explained why Ravage has been going to great lengths to avoid Hope all week long.

Under my stare, Ravage yanks his boots off the table and sits upright in his chair. "Yup, yup. We'll look into the guest list."

I glance farther down the table at Grinder. "Any thoughts, Father Grumpy?"

Grinder sits back and crosses his arms over his chest. "Keep calling me that, fucker. You're gonna find out how grumpy I can get."

"I think we're all aware," Z says.

"I'm with Mister Mouth." Grinder points at Teller. "Ran into a few folks who didn't seem to know how to act right."

Serena sits back and rubs her baby bump. Her forehead wrinkles for a second and she seems to be taking deep breaths.

"You okay, Serena?" I ask.

"Yes," she answers quietly.

"What's wrong," Grinder murmurs to her. The two of them bow their heads and whisper to each other.

Rock claps his hands to take the attention off of them. "Any other suggestions? Murphy, you've been awfully quiet."

"We missed most of the party." Murphy shrugs. "But

what we saw looked good." He glances at Heidi and raises an eyebrow.

"The new place is really great, Rav," Heidi adds with more enthusiasm than her husband. "I hope you saved all those decorations. The graveyard was perfect."

"We did!" Ravage sits up. "All boxed up in the basement for next year."

"Wrath?" Rock asks. "Thoughts?"

"You gonna let us borrow Furious again?" Dex asks.

The answer's yes. But I pretend to think it over. "I might be open to it."

Trinity smacks my leg. "You loved it."

"I loved your decorations." I nod to Bricks and farther down the table where Scribbles is sitting. "Jake and I made sure all your artwork was safely stored for next year."

"Thanks," Scribbles mumbles. Poor kid hates having attention on him.

"All right. I think we're done," Rock says. "Thanks, everyone."

The chatter increases as everyone breaks into smaller groups to catch up with each other.

I walk over to Rock and Hope's end of the table. "Why so quiet, Cinderella?"

She shrugs. "I think you covered all of it."

"Are you *suuuure*?" I ask, drawing out the question. "I'm surprised you didn't suggest better locks for the bedrooms at the new clubhouse."

She glares at me.

Rock kicks my leg.

"All right. Stop causing trouble." Trinity slides up next to me and takes my hand. "Time to go home."

"So soon, Angel Face?"

"Yes, Wrecking Ball."

"Before I wreck *you*," Rock warns.

Trinity and I circle the room, saying goodbye to everyone before leaving.

"Think you'll be an angel for me again next year?" I ask Trinity. "You kept that red suit, right?"

"Of course I did." She curls her arms around my forearm and snuggles up to my side. "I don't have to wait for Halloween to wear it again, though."

"How about now?"

"I could be convinced."

Together, we step out of the clubhouse and into the chilly November night and head toward home.

THE LOST KINGS MC® WORLD

By Autumn Jones Lake

SOMETIMES I'M ASKED WHERE THE STAND ALONE BOOKS fit into the Lost Kings MC World. This is a loose, chronological reading order that might help!

Suggested Chronological Reading Order

1. Kickstart My Heart (Hollywood Demons #1)
2. Blow My Fuse (Hollywood Demons #2)
3. Wheels of Fire (Hollywood Demons #3)
4. Renegade Path
5. Slow Burn (Lost Kings MC #1)
6. Corrupting Cinderella (Lost Kings MC #2)
7. Three Kings, One Night (Lost Kings MC #2.5)
8. Strength From Loyalty (Lost Kings MC #3)
9. Tattered on My Sleeve (Lost Kings MC #4)
10. White Heat (Lost Kings MC #5)
11. Between Embers (Lost Kings MC #5.5)

12. Bullets & Bonfires (Standalone)
13. More Than Miles (Lost Kings MC #6)
14. Warnings & Wildfires (Standalone)
15. White Knuckles (Lost Kings MC #7)
16. Beyond Reckless (Lost Kings MC #8)
17. Beyond Reason (Lost Kings MC #9)
18. One Empire Night (Lost Kings MC #9.5)
19. After Burn (Lost Kings MC #10)
20. After Glow (Lost Kings MC #11)
21. Zero Hour (Lost Kings MC #11.5)
22. Zero Tolerance (Lost Kings MC #12)
23. Zero Regret (Lost Kings MC #13)
24. Zero Apologies (Lost Kings MC #14)
25. Swagger and Sass (Lost Kings MC #14.5)
26. White Lies (Lost Kings MC #15)
27. Rhythm of the Road (Lost Kings MC #16)
28. Lyrics on the Wind (Lost Kings MC #17)
29. Diamond in the Dust (Lost Kings MC #18)
30. Crown of Ghosts (Lost Kings MC #19)
31. Throne of Scars (Lost Kings MC #20)
32. Reckless Truths (Lost Kings MC #21)
33. Deeper You Dig (Lost Kings MC #21.5)
34. Rust or Ride (Lost Kings MC #22)

...and many more to come...

AUTHOR NOTES

I hope you enjoyed this fun peek into the lives of the Lost Kings! I've been wanting to write a Halloween novella or short story collection for a while now. I finally said 2022 is the year it's going to happen.

And here we are!

Happy Halloween!

Autumn

www.ingramcontent.com/pod-product-compliance
Lightning Source LLC
Chambersburg PA
CBHW071526170626
46811CB00007B/2964

* 9 7 8 1 9 4 3 9 5 0 8 8 1 *